THE BLEEDING MAN
AND OTHER
SCIENCE FICTION STORIES

THE
BLEEDING MAN

and Other Science Fiction Stories

by **CRAIG STRETE**

with a foreword by Virginia Hamilton

GREENWILLOW BOOKS
A Division of William Morrow & Company, Inc.
New York

1   2   3   4   5   6   7   8   9   10

"The Bleeding Man" was first published by *Galaxy*.
"Into Every Rain, a Little Life Must Fall"
was first published by *Creative Computing*.

Story title spots adapted
from an illustration by Karl Stuecklen

Library of Congress Cataloging in Publication Data

Strete, Craig.   The bleeding man
and other science fiction stories.
Contents: The bleeding man.—Into every
rain, a little life must fall. [etc.]
1. Science fiction, American.   [1.
Science fiction.   2. Short stories]
I. Title.   PZ7.S9164Bi   [Fic]
77-4505   ISBN 0-688-80118-8
ISBN 0-688-84118-X lib. bdg.

Foreword

by Virginia Hamilton

SCIENCE FICTION, that realm of speculative writing in which the extravagantly fanciful is commonplace, generally anticipates world history by a few decades. SF writers have long worried over disappearing fossil fuels, overpopulation, global economic and military conflicts and nuclear disasters while we, the more fortunate of the world's people, daydreamed in overheated rooms. Now we've awakened to discover future shock at the foot of the sofa, while what was once SF fantasy is featured on the six o'clock news.

In this volume of six stories [entitled *The Bleeding Man*], Craig Strete takes a more subjective approach with his vision of lone individuals confronting worlds turned cold and impersonal. The first American Indian to become a successful Science Fiction writer, Strete frequently reflects his Amerind heritage in his stories, and concepts often are derived from that culture rather than from Western philosophy.

"I have sat on the good side of the fire. I have cried over young women. It is nothing but trouble." These words from the title story, "The Bleeding Man," have the controlled density of feeling and the touch of prophecy to be found in the best of Amerind literature.

All life is continuous, Craig Strete seems to be telling us, for time and again in these stories the dead walk the earth to speak to us, point the way, and, with the living, face the phantasmagoric.

"A Sunday Visit with Great-grandfather" is a wry, sagely comic tale in which a couple of space travelers have the utter misfortune to land on earth in the vicinity of great-grandson and his relatives.

"Into Every Rain, a Little Life Must Fall" is representative Science Fiction depicting a grim, urban civilization in which "wombcops" plugged into computer consoles monitor near-empty city streets from comfortable couches. They act as judge and jury with the power of life and death over the citizenry for infractions of an insane criminal code of law.

What is most impressive about this collection of stories is the wide range of Craig Strete's imaginative concerns and his ability to write difficult story ideas with brilliant clarity. The writing is smooth and unassuming, and yet the fabric of it is always richly textured.

Foreword

There are two stories—"White Brothers from the Place Where No Man Walks" and "The Bleeding Man"—in which the fictional fabric seems to be woven of meaning just beyond our reach. However, this other-worldliness should in no way affect our enjoyment. For Craig Strete has fused the ways of Amerind peoples to the realm of Science Fiction in a way that has never before been attempted.

Contents

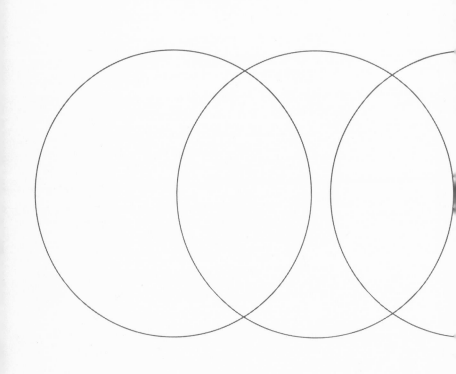

Into Every Rain, a Little Life Must Fall

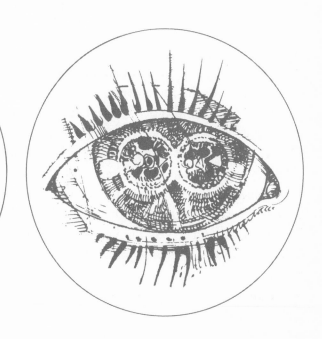

I PUNCHED into the console web, linked into the main computer. The control room was warm and comfortable, but outside it was a miserable night. The street monitors swept my sector and all of them shot back the same story. No action.

I'd lucked out on assignment. Hit the graveyard shift, which is my favorite. Most of the action breaks at night. Not this night, though.

It was cold and it was raining to beat hell and this was one of those kinds of night that give me the womb-cop blues.

The streets in my sector were deserted. Very depressing. I like action. I sat there behind my monitors, audio helmet jammed on my head, feeling like a football player sitting out a game on the bench.

I dialed Central to report myself in. "WOMBCOP 345-45. STEVENS, ROGER DAVIS. Reporting for duty, shift 2, punch in 0200, all systems functioning, nothing to report, no shift 1 carry-overs."

It was a slow night all over. I had only about half of my mobile street units out. Rain had the whole city locked in. It was coming down hard and cold and nobody in his right mind was out in it, or anyone in his wrong mind, either.

My hands itched with inaction, toying with the trigger grips of my bank of pocket lasers.

The rain had cut down visibility and I had all dispatched scanners turned up to the highest wide-angle scoop. Even then, my visual range was pretty limited.

I don't feel useful on a night like that. I like the action, like the feel of being on top of a crime, hitting into it, punching it in and putting it down. Then if I'm lucky, burning down. I wish there were some way of expressing the satisfaction I get when I burn down a criminal. I love my work.

Fifteen minutes plugged into the computer and not one peep.

Then action. "Position," said the computer. "Pick-up 27, Monitor 7."

This was more like it! I punched in video and audio and man, I felt alive again!

Nothing on audio but the sound of rain coming down on the pavement so hard it was bouncing. I tapped the toggle on my helmet. I was turning up to high again. Still nothing but the damn rain.

Visuals, the same story. A gray side street shrouded in rain. Couldn't pierce the rain more than ten feet at a time. I linked into the mobile unit. Scanners on high scope, still couldn't see a damn thing.

"27-7, move toward subject!" The monitor began moving down the street, rapidly.

The computer read out, "Pedestrian, unidentified racial type, unidentified gender. Computing."

"Identify," I snarled. I couldn't even begin to guess what was coming down.

The computer hesitated and then again, "Pedestrian, unidentified racial type, unidentified gender. Computing."

"Move in close, damn it!"

"Acknowledged."

I tapped the trigger grips impatiently. This seemed like it was taking forever. I felt like I was playing pin the tail on an invisible donkey.

Finally, audio picked up the sound of footsteps, the sound of feet splashing through puddles. A fraction of a second later, video picked out a bedraggled figure moving slowly through the rain. Heat scanners must have sensed him a long way off.

"Identify." The scanners freeze-framed his face, coded and transmitted the image automatically to Central.

"Caucasian, male. No information. No identity card, no arrest record. It does not compute."

Had to be a computer foul-up. Maybe fifty years ago it might have been possible for someone to exist without an identity card, but not anymore. Somebody in programming deserved a long vacation without pay.

"Pursue and monitor," I ordered, stalling until Central rang in with the correct information. That was the best I could do.

"It does not compute. Lack of data," clacked out Central.

"Telephoto zoom. Target: hands and fingers. Positive print I.D. check," I ordered the mobile unit, which immediately began circling subject, clicking extreme close-up telephoto freeze frames. I punched in the information direct to Central.

"Information acknowledged," read out Central. "No print record. Information does not compute."

What could I do? Damn programmers! I punched in. "Check programmer error!"

Central beat me to it. "Possibility programmer error eliminated. No identity card. No file tapes. Detain and identify. Violation of Identity Code, Section 348. Hold for questioning." One entire panel on my console lighted up. My computer units all locked into Central. They were functioning full gauge on this one. Damn!

I'd been a wombcop for ten years—ten years, and I'd never run into anyone who didn't have an identity card, who didn't have an identity tape on file! It's not only illegal, it's damn impossible! This was something new we had on our hands.

Two more panels switched in. The computer was going crazy on this one. As far as it was concerned, the impossible had happened.

I had my eyes riveted on my monitors and I was really giving our boy a looking over. He was no beauty.

"Detain." I punched in and the mobile unit that had been keeping pace with this character moved in and cuffed him to the detention cable on the side of the unit. No resistance, no reaction at all. Subject seemed unaware of the monitor circling around him.

It was an old man, video observation indicated. Frayed overcoat. He was about 1.63 meters tall, pants too big and ragged. Looked like an alcohol addiction case, a wino, unshaven. Eyes, on full zoom, looked bloodshot. He was unconcerned. Looked like he didn't care one way or the other about being stopped. Alcohol probable cause of brain damage indicated by subject's lack of interest, negative display of emotional response.

"Who are you? Please identify yourself?" My voice came through the mobile-unit speakers. Tapes being filed, a direct line to Central. All my panels were lighting up. My console looked like a computer light show. Central was really shooting sparks over this.

The old scarecrow looked directly into the monitor. Gaunt features, eyes sunk into his head. Deathly white face. I would have sworn I was talking to a corpse. No expression on the face, just kind of cold and withdrawn. No answer.

"Repeat. This is wombcop Davis. You are in violation of the Identity Code, Section 348. Please identify yourself."

Not a flicker of anything from the old man.

Central punched in. "Section Commander Hartmann on the line. What the blue hell is going on down there?"

I beeped in acknowledgment of his call.

"Checking, sir. We have a man with no identity records, sir."

"That's impossible!" Hartmann sounded fit to be deprogrammed.

"Please identify yourself?" I tried again. Jesus, this was really one for the tapes!

"Plug in your lie-detector monitors!" snapped Hartmann, his voice booming through loud on the line.

"They're already plugged in, sir! I can't get a response from subject, sir." Damn, I felt like an idiot. He knew I hadn't got a response, that order about the lie detector was just to prod me into getting one. This action was plugged into every section of Central. My console panels flashed with a thousand simultaneous plug-ins. Everybody was interested in this one.

My eyes stayed on the monitor. The old man turned away from the monitor and looked back over his shoulder, as if looking for someone, as if someone were following him.

"It's raining," said the old man. He turned around and looked straight into the monitor again.

I went to split screen, turned the console camera on me and put my picture in the bottom half of his screen. Standard interrogation procedure.

"This is wombcop Davis. You are in violation of . . . ."

He nodded once, rain pouring from the battered brim of his hat. "I know who you are."

"Please identify yourself." He could see me in his monitor, could see my hands resting lightly on the trigger grips of my pocket lasers. That threat gives me a psychological edge when questioning suspects. Seeing the burn-down triggers makes the threat more real to them.

No fear reaction in close-up video scan of his face. But there was something so strange about this old man that I found my own face tightening a little. I found my hands sweating on the trigger grips.

"Have you seen a man on this street? Did a man pass through here tonight?" asked the old man.

Stunned, I automatically shook my head no.

"Was you here last night? Did you see a man come through here last night? Did you see a man here after curfew?"

"Hartmann here." Audio cut in. "Play along with

him. Keep him talking. We've punched in voice prints, visual factors. We're running everything through the mill again. We have to have a computer error somewhere, possibly a circuit breakdown."

"I was on duty last night. I saw several men, but none after curfew. We had a woman after curfew, but no men," I answered, beeping in an affirmative to Commander Hartmann's call.

The old man's eyes burned in my monitor. The old man may have looked like a corpse but there was something fierce and wild about his eyes. They seemed to look right through me.

"Who are you looking for? Perhaps I can check with Central and locate him for you?"

He shook his head.

"I could send out a mobile unit to locate him for you."

"I'll find him first. I don't need you to find him. I'll find him first and then . . . ." He let the sentence trail off.

"Does this friend of yours have a name?" I asked, trying an indirect tack. If we could pin down an associate, maybe we could trace back to him.

"He's no friend of mine!" snarled the old man, an edge of violence in his voice. "I've got a *message* for him."

There was an unspoken threat in his manner, in the way he emphasized the word *message*.

"Perhaps we could help you deliver the message," I volunteered.

"No! Not yet. The only message I got for him is under my coat."

He tapped one of the bulky pockets of his overcoat.

I punched into the mobile unit, x-rayed him, scanned him with a metal detector. The unmistakable outline of a knife came from the pocket he had tapped with his unmanacled hand.

I debated immediate confiscation, but tabled it. As long as he was talking, and since he was manacled to the mobile unit and couldn't go anywhere, there was no sense in taking any overt action that might make him stop communicating. Nothing forced here, just playing along, hoping he would give out some useful information.

Central punched in again. "Hartmann here. There is no, repeat, *no* record of this man anywhere!" There was a note of panic in his voice. I could tell he was shook up and I didn't blame him. A contradiction like this could disrupt our entire society.

I wiped my hands against the armrests of my womb couch. I was sweating like a bandit caught on a monitor! At least this night wasn't boring anymore, I'll say that much. It was turning out to be one hell of a strange night.

The old man looked back over his shoulder again. He seemed to be waiting for someone.

I piped into Central with a query. "No possibility of programmer error?"

Hartmann punched right back. "None! We've checked and double-checked! We've got a file on every living human being! We've got everyone but him!" In the background of Hartmann's signal, I heard the sound of voices in heated argument.

"Who are you? Please identify yourself," I asked again, at Hartmann's insistent urging.

To my surprise, he told me.

"My name's Farris. Jonathan Farris." Again the old man looked back the way he had come, and shivered in the rain. He was cold and wet and miserable. If there hadn't been something so wrong with him—so *evil* is the word I guess I'm looking for—maybe I would have felt a little bit of pity for the old man. But there was something very wrong with this old man, something terrible and grim which stopped any pity I might have felt toward him. Besides, I'm a wombcop. I don't have much pity for anything or anybody.

"Shall I bring him in?" I queried Central.

Before I got an answer the old man spoke again.

"Bantam is his name. Michael Bantam is the one I'm looking for. He's behind me, I'm sure. I might have passed him in the rain, but he'll be along."

"Checking on Bantam," clacked my computer link-up.

"I've got to meet him. You've got to let me go," said the old man, shaking his manacled hand. "I'll be late and I mustn't be late." A shadow of worry moved across his haggard face.

"But . . . ," I started to say through the mobile speakers.

"Release him immediately!" Hartmann's terse command snapped across the relays. "Have him followed! We want a record of everyone he meets, file tapes on everything he does or says!"

My hand jumped off the console board, curling into a fist with shock. I was stunned by the command, which was contrary to everything I had ever been taught. I've never let a violator go free! Not once in ten years! Not once!

"Damn it, Davis! That's a direct order! Snap to it!"

I shook myself into action, punched in the release command. I had a sick sensation in the pit of my stomach as my fingers tapped in the order. This was contrary to everything I stood for, everything I believed in.

The manacle automatically came unsnapped. The old man nodded his head and backed away from the mobile unit, massaging his freed wrist.

"At least let me confiscate the illegal concealed weapon?" I asked Central. "My God, I can't let . . . ."

"Denied." Central's reply was immediate.

"You're free to go," I heard myself say. My hands shook on the console and I fought with myself to keep from automatically reaching for the laser triggers. My mind was crying for a burn-down. My trigger fingers twitched instinctively.

"I've got to get going. He'll be coming along and I've got to find him," said the old man, touching his overcoat pocket. "If you see him, you tell him that Jonathan Farris is going to get him. I'll see him killed for what he did to me."

"What does he look like? How will I know him when I see him?" I asked.

On a monitor beside my head, a series of telephoto stills of Michael Bantam appeared on the screen, piped in direct from Central. As the series of photographs flashed across the screen, biographical information automatically printed out across the bottom half of the screen. Central's computers were really on the ball.

"You'll know him when you see him," said the old man with a smile that had no smile to it. "He's young, red hair cut short. There's a scar over his left eye and his face is pale like dirty newspaper. You'll know him when you see him. He'll be coming along grinning, he'll be laughing at me, but not for long." Again the old man let his hand rest meaningfully on his overcoat pocket.

"If I see him, I'll tell him you're looking for him," I assured him. I glanced at the monitors. A pretty accurate description the old man gave. At least there was a record of Michael Bantam.

Why the hell was I letting him go? What the hell was going on down at Central? Had they gone soft in their computer programs? I slammed my fist down on the console, punching in angrily to Central. I was going to get some answers! I'd had about all I could take. I didn't know what the hell was going on. This man was a criminal whether he was on file or not, and I had every right to burn him down.

I started to speak, but the old man cut in and I listened and waited, choking on my own anger and frustration.

"He'll never get away with it! Nobody does that to me and gets away with it! I'll see him dead before the night is gone." The old man was livid with rage.

The circuit-monitoring panels were all flashing emergency reds and I knew the computer system was pushing toward an overload.

I punched a sharp query at Central. "What the god damn . . . ?"

"Why don't you follow me?" said the old man, beckoning the mobile unit toward him. "Just down this street and left a little ways down the alley. Yes, why don't you follow me?" He began walking.

I looked at my sector chart. The alley was the cut-off point at the end of my patrol sector. That was someone else's territory. I punched in this information. Awaited a go-ahead.

"Hartmann here. Ignore boundaries. Follow without

restriction or limitation. Full monitoring, automatic filing, total surveillance."

I shrugged. It was a day for breaking the rules. I activated the mobile unit and it began tracking and pursuing the old man. Together, they moved down the street toward the alley.

I started to beep in an acknowledgment of the order.

Suddenly, everything went dead. Console, monitors, link-ups, activation circuits. Everything. Nothing coming in, nothing going out. Computer overload. It had to be. The existence of the old man with no identity records, with no file tapes, was an insoluble problem. It wasn't supposed to be possible.

The womb couch cradled me like a hand, the release catches that would free me from its comfortable grip frozen into place by the power failure. I sat in the dark, felt like a helpless stuffed animal in the hands of a child.

I never felt so useless in my life. I struggled against the lock in the couch web, trying to force it manually, but it was impossible to shake loose. I was stuck there, helpless, like a butterfly stuck to a display board with a pin.

I shouted my frustrations at the darkened console in front of me. There was nothing I could do but wait. Nothing, not one damn thing!

It wasn't a minor overload. It must have been the granddaddy of granddaddies. My entire sector, from street unit to computer master terminal, had blanked. Whoever was responsible for programming a computer solution on this case ought to get burned down. It was an error on the scale of programming a computer to find the square root of zero! Somebody was going to be up the computer without a program!

There must have been one hell of a lot of damage to repair. My wrist chronometer wasn't working. Just guessing, I'd say I sat there maybe an hour or more. Probably closer to two.

The power came back on around 0418 hours. Maybe 0419.

Central was on the line while I was still blinking my eyes, trying to adjust to the console lights when they flashed back on.

Commander Hartmann's voice almost broke my eardrums. I winced under my audio helmet and turned down the audio pick-up.

"WHAT'S HAPPENING DOWN THERE?" he demanded.

I rubbed my eyes, waiting for them to adjust. The monitors were flashing back on, focusing and retuning for maximum image clarity.

"Locate Pick-up 27, Monitor 7," I shouted. The monitor for 7 had not focused properly yet. The blurred pattern on the monitor merged and then refocused. The forward progress of the mobile unit that had been assigned to the suspect had been stopped dead in its tracks just as it was turning into the alley. When the power surged on, the unit completed the turn, its scanners probing the alley.

"Position," clacked the computer. "Pick-up 27, Monitor 7."

Mobile unit moved forward into the alley, scanners set. Audio punched in.

Tapes were filing. Red flash on my console. Mobile unit activated an emergency panel. Other units from other sectors were on standby with possible intercept patterns.

There was a body in the center of the alley. My mouth dropped open in shock. The computer frantically began absorbing data, counter-referencing, automatic alert all sectors.

That haggard face, the sunken eyes, the old coat. A knife sticking out of the old man's chest. Unmistakable.

I went to full zoom, extreme close-up, lateral pan. Very clearly marked. A color-coded homicide tag attached to the handle of the knife. I punched in for a close-up on the card. It told me that the victim was murdered, unmonitored, discovered by first shift of sector eight, assignment G, shift one carry-over, that the body was overdue for pick-up by sanitation. There was a blue sticker on the end of the tag that meant preserve body for evidence, autopsy mandatory.

Sweet Jesus!

The computer read out, "DECEDENT . . . FARRIS, JONATHAN FRANKLIN, MALE. CAUCASIAN. AGE 57. BIRTH-

DATE 2053/03.09. CAUSATION: Knife wound through right ventricle. ESTIMATED TIME EXPIRATION . . . 3 hours, 27 minutes, 55 seconds when first discovered. UPDATE EST. T. EXP. this scan: 6 hours, 19 minutes, 31 seconds. DEATH . . . instantaneous. CONCLUSION . . . HOMICIDE. MOTIVES . . . UNKNOWN. SUSPECTS . . . UNKNOWN. Actual crime unmonitored. No more information available without request through proper channels to sector 8. Case jurisdiction . . . sector 8. System breakdown, factor in loss of information. Suggest alternate . . . ."

I cut the computer off and sat on the switch that hooked me into Central. Commander Hartmann appeared on a video monitor to my right. My console camera automatically plugged me into his office.

We just sat there and stared at each other, too shocked to even speak. I felt sick, physically sick.

"When a man dies, they take his identity file off record," said Commander Hartmann. His face was pale with shock. "The computer was able to correctly identify Farris. . . ."

"But . . . ," I started to say.

"From information already on file in the Death Register," he continued.

I got a cold feeling in the pit of my stomach.

"Are you trying to tell me the reason we couldn't get a make on him is because he was already dead? Are you saying he was dead when I picked him up in my sector? That we had no tape records of him because his files listed him as deceased?"

Commander Hartmann shuddered and stared down at the blank surface of his desk. "I don't have an explanation. I'm not sure I want one. Christ! Christ!" A nervous tic jerked one side of his face grotesquely. He was struggling to maintain his grip on reality.

Jesus! I turned away from Hartmann's monitor and stared at the corpse of Farris.

"He was dead three hours before I punched into my shift! But . . . but . . . ." Words failed me. I couldn't move, couldn't think. I sat in my womb couch, paralyzed.

I'm just a wombcop, an extension of my computers, the driver of the car. My job's driving, punching in and doing what I'm trained for, not explaining the engine. This was out of my league. I only know what the computers know. Then I act on it. That's my job. That's all I want to do.

Commander Hartmann was on the edge of hysteria.

"Command decision!" he ordered, his voice ragged. It was a direct order.

I was confused. Hell, I was scared. I was terrified. I knew the decision he expected me to make. I just sat there stunned. I wanted to pretend I couldn't hear him, to pretend that I didn't know what the hell he was talking about.

"I SAID COMMAND DECISION!" repeated Hartmann, shouting, his voice cracking with emotion.

I punched into Central, pressed the automatic filing code. I tried to stay calm but my hands shook as I dialed in.

It was the hardest thing I ever did, the most difficult command decision I ever made.

My voice sounded distant and cold, as if it belonged to someone else as I punched in the only command decision I could possibly make. "ARREST MICHAEL BANTAM FOR THE MURDER OF JONATHAN FARRIS. CAPTURE AND EXECUTE ON SIGHT. VIOLATION OF CRIMINAL CODE, SECTION 81-4. THIS IS A PRIORITY COMMAND. IMPLEMENT IMMEDIATELY."

The report went to Central. The first time, I hope the only time in my life, I had made a decision that wasn't based on cold hard facts. You tell me what my decision was based on. An eyewitness account of a murder from the victim? I'm not sure I know.

I waited for a decision from Central. They had all the evidence I had. Trouble was, the information I acted on would never compute, and I knew it. They could have my head for a thing like that. I was a mass of jelly, a shock cube of raw nerves, waiting, just waiting.

The seconds crawled by slowly. I could feel the sweat pouring from me, seeping into the soft cushion of the womb couch at my back. An hour went by like an eternity bathed in my own sweat.

Central linked up. "SUBJECT: COMMAND DECISION OF WOMBCOP 345-45 STEVENS, ROGER DAVIS, CASE NUMBER 87-411a (SECTOR 8, JURISDICTION SUPERCEDED, APPROVED TRANSFER COMMAND DECISION TO SECTOR 7) HOMICIDE, DECISION ON APPREHENSION AND EXECUTION OF MICHAEL BANTAM . . . ."

There was a pause. Oh God, no, I thought, here it comes . . .

Central continued, "APPROVED. MICHAEL BANTAM APPREHENDED SECTOR 9. EXECUTED FOR VIOLATION OF CRIMINAL CODE, SECTION 81-4. CONFIRMED. SPECIAL CITATION OF MERIT ISSUED THIS DATE, WOMBCOP 345-45 STEVENS, ROGER DAVIS, FOR INDIVIDUAL EFFORT WITHOUT AID OF COMPUTER ASSISTANCE. . . . CONGRATULATIONS."

What really happened that rainy night? I'm not sure I really want to know. As a very good computer friend of mine once said, it simply does not compute.

White Brothers from the Place Where No Man Walks

ONE EVENING Old Coat sat down in the fire. He did not wince or move his face. After a while the fire burned low. No one spoke.

Old Coat's daughter sat in the cornfield. Within her belly her sorrowing boy child knew it would be born dead.

Uzmea the conjurer came in the night. Uzmea, the throat spreader, killed her and put her head in a red clay pot. Now the story begins.

Uzmea the taker of sacrifices lived in a cave of no color. No warrior went seeking Uzmea. He lived in the mountains among the strange gods and devices of his race.

One day of blackness and ground clouds, Uzmea

came into Chota and stood silently by the village house. Warriors, women and small ones gathered around him. No one dared move too close, for it was rumored that arms would drop from hands that touched Uzmea.

Uzmea had lived in the place of no color longer than the memory of the pretty women. He had been with our people from back into the time of the big cold land. He was not of our way. He wore strange plates of yellow metal around his chest. Upon his head was a strange metal shield with a tall bird plume. Around his neck was a string of glass stones that were red and blue and glitter. He worshiped strange gods. Gods of the sky and another more powerful, a snake god with feathers.

Twice had Uzmea come into Chota. Twice had the ground shaken the roots of houses and trees down. Twice water in the river had risen and fallen like the tide of the big water, the bottoms of lakes became hills, the earth cracked with the great wounds and the hot foul breath of demons went into the air.

And each time Uzmea had spoken in a strange tongue to the sun. And then to us he spoke of this world-shake. It was a warning that the land would have new masters, Uzmea said.

Now Uzmea stood in the village again. Many hearts were tight with fear. Uzmea spoke to the sun in his strange tongue. Then he turned to the real people and said in our tongue, "Listen and I shall tell you of a time long ago. I am the not-alive and the not-dead. I came to this place many animal ages ago. I made prophecy that the great white brothers would come. For the Delawares were upon you and your fires had sunk low. I told your oldest fathers of this place and of the coming of the white brothers who would keep your fires high. And I took blood that my prophecy would grow.

"It was many lifetimes before the whites came. They were not the white brothers I had prophesied. These white men came in ships across the big water. Uzmea sat in his cave dreaming and waiting. The real people had forgotten him except in fire talk, but Uzmea did not forget.

"These white men became your brothers, but they were not the white brothers of the time of need. Once again I spoke to the oldest of your fathers. I said, The white man will take your land. He will point you to the West, but there is no home for you there. He will make you become like him. He will say your way is no good. He will make roads across your heart so that he may come and look at you. He will teach you his tongue and the strange markings that are his you will learn. He will teach your people to spin and weave clothes that cover what you are not. He will teach you not to hunt and not to fight but to take food out of the ground. By these means he will destroy. He will marry your women and the children will be born boneless and bloodless.

"Some believed Uzmea and some did not. Hide, my children. Go to sleep, I said. Those who believed Uzmea hid in the caves and the high places. They stayed pure. Today I have come to this gathering place for the last time.

"In the eyes of the whites, you are outlaws, the ones who did not move West. Your bones are strong and your blood sings. I have seen the clearness, the vision. I shall speak this once and go to the cave of my race for all time. I have seen the white brother who is yet to come. Perhaps he will come quickly or not in your breathing time. Time has no feeling to him. Years are days to this white brother. But come now or for your children he will know your need. He will look upon your bodies that are thin with hair. He will look at the blood of your children and it shall be his blood.

"His ways are strange, but that which was taken from you the white brother will give back. He is mighty. He comes across the place where no man walks. Give him the strange things of the ground so that your brothers may live and breed in his home far from this place. This is my prophecy."

Then Uzmea beckoned with his hand to Old Coat.

Old Coat did not show fear as he walked toward Uzmea. He was walking to his death, he knew.

Uzmea stared at Old Coat with ugly prophecy eyes

and raised his hands in front of his unsleeping eyes. Old Coat stood before Uzmea. He looked straight into Uzmea's eyes, his back straight. Uzmea's hands fell upon Old Coat's face and Old Coat became as one dead. His eyes were dead fisheyes in his head.

"Do you see?" asked Uzmea.

Old Coat's voice came from the faraway of the grave. "I see."

Uzmea drew his robe about him. "Three deaths will feed this dream. Three blood lifes will grow my prophecy."

As swift as hawk shadow, Uzmea went away from them and disappeared into the hill trees.

Old Coat stood on his dead legs. He began walking with stiffness and the real people parted and let him pass. He went to his house and called his daughter's name. She lay within, heavy with child. She came out and many were the people who gave moan. For she was dead, too.

Old Coat and his dead daughter stood in front of the council fire. Old Coat lifted his arms and pointed at the lights in the sky. "They are there," his voice said. "The home of the white brothers is in the sky. The stars are their home. They shall come in round pots through the place where no man walks. They shall give the false white brother the sickness and he will wither as in winter. We will live as we did before. The prophecy is spoken. We must fall asleep and wait and watch the sky."

That night Old Coat sat down in the fire. He did not wince or move his face. After a while the fire burned out. No one spoke.

Old Coat's daughter sat in the cornfield. Within her belly, her sorrowing boy child knew it would be born dead.

Uzmea the conjurer came in the night and killed her and put her head in a red clay pot. He set the pot high in the mountains. Her eyes were pointed to the stars to guide the white brothers through the place where no man walks. No one speaks of this. They are all asleep. Uzmea alone is awake. Uzmea waits and watches beneath the stars.

The story has begun.

When They Find You

IT WAS strange and spring and the clouds did barrel rolls overhead. He awoke before dawn and went into the empty room where his waking life lived. The glassless windows brought the cool winds of the twin moon season into the room and a chill worked into him slowly, a sleepless chill that moved through him.

He faced himself in the shaving mirror and remembered how it had been. There had been a time when he had taken pride in his aloneness, in having no people of his own kind closer than fifty miles away. But the dark-eyed young man he now faced in his mirror had been made over, had been changed by something deep and restless within him. Five years of

the new world, five years alone without the compli-
cation of living with other human beings.

He rolled his tongue over his lips uneasily, disturbed
by an unfamiliar taste, and his hand unconsciously
strayed to his cheek in an imagined caress.

Behind the cabin, the stefel dogs moved restlessly
on poison-tipped spines in the corral. They were
strangely sensitive to the moods of those around them,
and now they shifted nervously, coiling and uncoiling
spinal tendrils in flowing sheaves around their brain
pouches. Their seasonal restlessness matched his own.

Gantry moved through the doorless cabin entrance,
picking up the feeding pails near the door. The metal
armor on his legs clanked together as he walked. At
the sound of his approach, the stefel dogs began
moving together in the center of the corral. They
massed their coils around a central core, forming an
interwoven tube dangling into the air like a cannon
barrel.

Gantry moved into the feeding shed near the corral
and emerged with two pails of honey heavily laced
with potassium cynanide. The tube widened at the
end as he leaned the bucket over the rail of the metal
fence. The poison spines hissed through the air, beat-
ing against the fence at him. The spines bounced off
his leg armor. One spine grazed the bucket, nearly
hitting his hand. He jumped back with a curse, nearly

dropping the bucket. The spines were instantly fatal. It was the second time in three weeks that he had come near to getting stung. I'm getting careless, he told himself; either that, or I don't care anymore.

He put the bucket back to the fence, being a little more careful where he placed his hands this time. The tube of coiled tendrils widened even further as he poured the sweet poison down the fleshy straw the stefel dogs had formed. The honey mixture ran slowly down the tube and the blue beasts began the first color change, turning a faint green as the poison began working through the cellular walls.

It took a long time for the bucket to empty and it gave him time to think. His thoughts turned to the time when he had come here. Five years ago he had been a different person and this world had been all new to him. The call for volunteers, for pioneers, had come and Gantry had been the restless type, filled with a burning itch for something different. He'd been one of the first to sign up, one of the first colonists to settle on Kingane planet, and for five years he had had no regrets.

He was twenty-four when he landed, impatient of the stay-at-home life he had left on earth. He had come here hoping to rid himself forever of the settled ways of his own kind.

But in the end of his fifth year, as he tended his herd of stefel dogs under the twin moons, a dissatisfaction and a longing began in him that made his steps slow and uncertain. There was no longer any pleasure in the long stretches of Kingane summers, summers that brought the darbyo birds across the sky, circling in complicated patterns above. Beautiful creatures they were, fire red and snow white, silent like flights of dreams, wheeling like specters across the twilight skies.

But now the coming of the winter and the pebble storms oppressed him. The weather was always mild in the dead of winter and though the storms, really meteor-fragment showers, were short, it was necessary to stay inside for the two months of winter. He had faced four winters without incident, exercising daily, planning the new buildings, the stefel dog barn he knew he would someday build. But now this spring, winter yet five months away, he was already looking toward the next winter with a feeling of being trapped within himself.

He made good money, more than was quite decent, he sometimes thought. And with that money, he'd filled his empty cabin with things, amusements, books, that occupied him for a little while. Stefel dogs, carefully tended until they reached four and one half months old, and then poisoned with potassium cynanide, produced a very fine crop of nerve tissue—nerve tissue unlike human tissue in that it could regenerate. It had become the most important discovery of the five new worlds. It made him a rich man and kept the idle rich on earth very, very young. A rich man would pay plenty for a stefel-tissue transplant. The stefel tissue replaced nerve tissue, replicating the exact genetic structure and information encoded on the decaying nerve tissue it replaced. A small transplant of stefel tissue eventually replaced the entire cellular structure of a man's brain, becoming an effectual replacement immune to the ravages of time and able to regenerate itself constantly.

It was the discovery of the stefel dogs that had given man the promise of immortality. Before stefel transplants, the ability to synthesize organs had increased the life span of man to two hundred years. They had synthetic hearts, synthetic lungs, livers, all the organs, even veins, arteries and skin. All these things had been possible because they could implant grafts taken from each of these organs and grow them in nutrient plastic, shaping them into new organs tougher than the old ones. But the one thing beyond man's capabilities was the ability to regenerate brain and nerve tissue. They could slow down the aging process but they could not stop it entirely, not until Kingane planet opened itself to colonists and the hardy settlers discovered the stefel dogs.

The tube had filled with the honey mixture and the second color change began. Gantry watched them carefully. It was important that they not separate until he was sure they had each absorbed enough of the poison. His first year there, they had separated too quickly and the pools of nerve tissue that the stefel dogs degenerated into at death had been contaminated with unconverted brain tissue, an unpleasant experience and a very costly one. The unoxidized brain tissue began forming into crippled stefel dogs, crying piteously through their half-formed air sacs, fouling the nerve tissue with tiny synaptic runners expanded through the pools of oxidized material.

One of the tendrils near the rim of the feeding tube began fluttering, beginning to uncoil. Just narrowly missing the waving rows of poisonous spines that clattered up at him, Gantry ran his hand around the rim of the tube. His quick movement enticed the creatures into thinking that more food was coming down the tube. The tendril curled back into position as his hand made a complete circuit of the tube rim. Gantry moved his hand away, satisfied that the tendrils would stay in place long enough to allow enough poison through to complete the process.

He turned away from the creatures, absorbed in his thoughts, and walked back into the feeding shed. The sound of the generators kicking on caused a ripple in the brain-pouch fabrics of the stefel dogs. The vibration of the pump engines that kicked on as soon as the generators had reached a sufficient level to run them caused boil-like corrugations across the flat surfaces of the creatures' hairless bodies. The eyestalks began receding, settling into the folds of flesh above the exposed air sacs that flowed freely across the surface of the squat, now blue-gray creatures.

Gantry emerged from the building dragging a flexible length of tubing obviously connected to the machines within the interior of the feeding shed. There was a nozzle attached to the end of the hose, and a thin metal tube with a rubberoid bulb attached dangled from a point about five inches away from the end of the tubing.

Gantry climbed over the low corral bars and moved toward the low end of the corral. The floor of the corral was made of hard-formed plastic, tilted at an angle, divided by a shallow trench around the outside of the enclosure that also bisected the middle of the corral. Mindful of the swinging poison spines reaching out toward him, Gantry inserted the hose in a groove fitted to the side of the center pool. The end of the tubing dangled into the center of the trench. He squeezed the bulb several times to force air out of the line.

Already the tube of the dogs was beginning to fold in on itself. The air sacs began sinking into the skin as the structures that held them in place began dissolving. The blood-red color of the last change suffused through the dying creatures like a dying sunset. There was a hissing, melting sound and Gantry sensed a harsh, unpleasant chemical tang to the air.

It was this part of the process that had always disturbed him. It was the alienness of the creatures that bothered him. Their silence, their lack of struggle. A kind of alien intelligence that seemed in no way affected by external circumstance, yet was sensitive to things like fear, loneliness and restlessness, but contained no seeming awareness of its own destruction. At times Gantry was convinced that the creatures were humoring him, as if they were somehow above mortal considerations. Once when he had taken ill, he'd found them clustered sympathetically around the front entrance of his cabin, their poison spines folded inward inoffensively. Of course it was only his impression of them, but they seemed to radiate emotions, to be sensitive to things around them. How they had crawled out of their pen without the legs that were removed surgically at birth, he never knew. He was positive he had sensed their concern, intuited it from the waving motions of the spinal tendrils. It had been an unnerving experience, one that had remained with him.

For a long time after that, he had had dreams about the creatures, about them surprising him one night as he slept—falling upon him, wrapping his face up in their tendrils, covering his body in the dark with the slick, ropy nerve endings, tightening, suffocating him with their combined weight, choking him with their thick, yellow bodily excretions, flaying his body with their razor-sharp poison spines.

The first stream of oxidized nerve tissue began trickling down the narrow trench in the floor of the enclosure. It was like a semi-thick soup, discolored, running slowly. Gantry released the handle on the nozzle and the hose began sucking in air. Satisfied that his work was finished, he left the corral and went to the big storage tanks behind the corral. The tanks were partially filled with liquid nitrogen, a perfect refrigerant for the nerve tissue that would soon be flowing into the tanks. He checked the gauges in the tanks. They were satisfactory.

The screaming began and Gantry knew it was time to leave. The screaming was not really unpleasant. It was rather melodious, a sort of birdlike trill as the air sacs began disintegrating, but still he knew it for what it was—the death rattle of the creatures—and he was in no mood to listen to that. He moved away from the cabin, heading down the hill toward the sulfur water spring.

A family of Riyall were there before him. The Riyall were the native race of Kingane, strange, aloof peoples, divided into many different tribes. There were very few of them left. Diseases, unknown to Kingane before the coming of Earth people, had taken whole groups of them. And then there had been fighting when many of the more highly civilized of the wild Riyalls had put up a fight against the encroachments on their land. The first year Gantry had set down on Kingane he'd signed up in the militia, had engaged in several skirmishes with the revolting Riyall bands and had personally killed several of them. He neither liked nor disliked them. They were humanoid, so genetically close to humans that it only required minor genetic surgery to make intermarriage possible. A thing that some of the settlers had been doing, as the loneliness of a world without women of their own kind weighed heavily upon them. It was not until his third year that the danger was really over. The last of the big Riyall bands had been exterminated then, leaving him free to spend all his time raising stefel dogs and building a small empire on the new world. Even now, there were occasional incidents, cases where travelers had been found dead, horribly disfigured by the Riyalls.

It was therefore with some caution that he advanced toward the spring. He had left the house without his hand weapons. He had long since stopped wearing a gun, the years of peace seemingly canceling the need for it.

They were aware of his coming, had been a minute before he was aware that they were even there. It was a big family group, one of the largest he'd seen in the last year or so. There were about thirty adults, a dozen or so young children and a good-sized group of teen-aged youngsters. The group moved away from the water hole as he approached, falling silently back as he reached the spring.

Gantry raised his hand and drew one finger across his bared teeth. It was the sign that meant he came in peace. He moved down by the spring. They stared at him silently, expressionlessly, as he cupped his hands in the water and drank his fill from the sulfurous water.

Suddenly, as if they had all reached the same decision, they moved back toward the water, careful to maintain a guarded distance between themselves and Gantry. Gantry sat back on his heels and watched them drinking, filling their lizard-bladder containers with water of the spring. They were uninhibited peoples, both sexes stripping their animal-hide clothes off to slide into the water of the spring. Having decided to ignore him, the young ones were already playing and splashing in the water.

Gantry watched them, watched as even the old ones got caught up in a water-splashing fight. And he envied them. They were simple people, always moving, rather childlike in their ways. The sight of a gray-haired old woman, naked as the day of her birth, splashing like a five-year-old child, filled him with a kind of vicarious pleasure and at the same time, a feeling that he was being left out.

His eyes appraised them. They were short, wiry people about 1.73 meters on the average. They had white skin running to a very dark reddish yellow. There seemed to be a great deal of variety from one group to the next. Some groups, like the one before him, had orange hair mixed with black, a strange coloration he found not at all displeasing. Their faces were basically human with the exception that facial expressions were not possible. Their faces were flat-planed. They could neither smile nor frown, lacking the facial muscles for either task. Neither could they close their eyelids or dilate their eyes. Their eyes were the most disturbing feature. They had twin pupils, only one of which functioned in the day, while both functioned in the dark. They had a way of staring, enhanced by their lack of facial expressions and their lidless eyes, that was unnerving.

They dressed plainly, wearing cured animal hides, mostly those of the snowfur lizards that lived in the mountain regions, although occasionally one would have a shirt made of darbyo skin, ornately beaded with darbyo bones. Their only weakness seemed to be for shiny metal, which they pounded into bracelets, items highly prized by the Riyall as having magic properties that would aid the wearer.

Then too, they had a fondness for alcohol, a fondness that led them to great misfortune since the Riyall did not have the proper enzymes to ingest alcohol. A small shot of whiskey was enough to make the strongest of their number drunk. For one of them to drink half a bottle would be fatal, a thing that the early colonists soon discovered and used to great effect against the natives in the early stages of the war.

Gantry's eyes were attracted to a young girl standing beside the spring. She was beautiful even by earth standards. Her skin was almost white, with a deeper hue of red-yellow. Her body was sleek, with almost a golden quality in the Kingane sun. She shook her body luxuriously, unselfconsciously, casting off a fine spray of water from the tawny orange-black mane of hair that hung well past her shoulders. And as he looked at her, the source of his restlessness became clear to him.

As self-sufficient as he prided himself on being, he could not quell the feelings that come to a lonely man, to a man who looks in the mirror one morning, realizing somewhere deep inside that he doesn't want to grow old alone.

In his heart, watching her move along the edge of the spring, he felt the meaning of the word freedom slipping away. He felt things stirring within him he had long since thought dead, buried. His pride had cut him off from family, from settling down, but now he felt a stealing tide of emotion slipping over his being, and in that instant, he knew he was lost.

He rose slowly and approached an old man who had not entered the water. He was the leader, an old man with one eye gone, a thick strip of lizard hide wrapped around his head, covering the old wound.

"Do you speak English?" asked Gantry.

The old man, watching the young ones at their play, did not turn to look at him. He grunted once, affirmatively.

Gantry stared at the young girl. She was unmarried. The married Riyall woman wore a leather strip dyed blue around one ankle. Her ankles were bare. Gantry figured her to be somewhere around sixteen or seventeen. He kept his eyes on her, the words he knew he would speak damming up in his throat in a tumbled stream.

The old man turned to look at Gantry, fixing him with his expressionless Riyall stare.

And in that moment, as he turned to look at the old man, turned and looked, he was almost able to stop himself. He remembered the times he had sworn to the buyers who came to buy his stefel harvest, sworn to them that he'd never touch a Riyall woman. Call it racial prejudice, or simply racial fear, he'd sworn he'd never degrade himself with a Riyall woman. He'd always told himself the colony company would get white women moved in some day, always told himself he could wait until then. He was about to make a liar out of himself.

Five years he'd waited, five years while the colony company had promised women were coming. They were a long time coming and there were a lot of men, men like Droble who lived fifty miles from Gantry,

Droble with two Riyall women, who couldn't wait.

"I want her," said Gantry, the words finally coming out.

"She—daughter—oldest—of mine," said the old man, in broken English.

"How much?" asked Gantry, committed to it now.

Not knowing the word, the old one pointed at Gantry's chest. "Bkaksi!" said the old man, and he turned his head and motioned at the girl. She came up to his side and he said several words to her in his own language. She took the news calmly, standing silently by the old man, gazing at Gantry with that dead, expressionless Riyall look on her face.

Gantry did not understand.

"How much?" repeated Gantry, and he tried to indicate by gestures that he wanted her.

The old man nodded and touched his own chest. He fingered his snowfur lizard shirt and pointed at Gantry's chest.

"That," said the old man, and he made smoothing motions along his shoulders and arms.

"The shirt?" asked Gantry, fingering the heavy work shirt. He made a gesture as if taking it off and offering it to him.

The old man nodded and pushed her toward him. She walked toward him and stood beside him, turning to face her father.

Gantry pulled the shirt off over his head and handed

it over. The old man took it, folded it several times, laid it upon the ground, arranging it carefully, and then sat down on it. He then turned away from them, the matter dismissed from his mind.

Gantry stood there for a little while, the enormity of what he had just done finally sinking in. He turned to look at the young Riyall girl beside him. She did not seem upset or nervous. It seemed to be of little importance to her, taking the fact of her having to go with him as a matter over which she had no control.

Gantry turned and began walking away, the Riyall girl moving along behind him, following five paces behind as was customary in her culture. The walk back to the cabin seemed to last an eternity to Gantry, who seemed to be in a kind of shock, filled with an irrational fear. He had no idea what to expect from her. No idea then, but he soon found out.

She was more than he had ever expected. At first, he told himself, it was sex that had prompted him to buy her, that he was not lonely, but even that lie fell away. He was lonely, and she filled that void. She wasn't human. He could never quite think of her that way, never get involved with her, he told himself, but there were times when the difference seemed small, insignificant.

Although she seemed to show no emotions of her own, she was quick to perceive his. She seemed in some strange way related to the stefel dogs, having that kind of sensitivity, a turning outward with little directed at herself. She seemed to accept things passively—her personality suited to fit him and not her. She seemed to honor him and respect him in ways he himself could not quite understand. Her body seemed to exist to please him, her hands so soft and yielding in his, at times playful, coy almost when she sensed he needed some kind of resistance, when she sensed he needed something to oppose him.

But she had a will of her own in matters that did not directly affect him. He had discovered with a kind of shock that the trade, that the ceremony of giving a shirt for her was as binding as any marriage ceremony on any of the planets. And one day, why he never knew, after six months of their being together, after six months of sharing the same bed, he loaded her in the all-terrain vehicle and took her the 420 kilometers to the nearest hospital, and there, he had her placed in surgery, so that she might have his children. What drove him to that, he could never quite say. It was not something he was sure he wanted for himself. In fact, the idea filled him with a kind of quiet terror. As if a child would be proof of his crime, a crime that was no crime on Kingane, but an act that still disturbed his spirit, that troubled his sleep as she lay beside him.

In a way, he supposed, in some sort of meaningfully twisted way, he was doing it for her, as if he was fulfilling some sort of obligation to her.

He remembered how she had touched him as the doctors wheeled her away to surgery and he had been reminded of a dog that one sends to a vet to have put to sleep. In that blank stare of hers, so guileless, so direct, he saw the pet dog, unsuspecting, trusting perfectly in your love even up until that moment when the needle breaks the skin and the long sleep begins.

In spite of his toughness he found tears in his eyes. The wrongness of his actions sat very heavily upon him, and deep inside, trapped within as deeply as he was trapped without, he knew he had as much power to stop it as he had to stop the clouds overhead.

The trip back to the cabin was a silent one, an uneasy trip, with Gantry sitting as far away from her as possible. He knew she was in pain, but he could not bring himself to touch her, to offer her any comfort. He was not so sure, now that she was fertile, now that he had made it possible for them to have children, if he did not hate her. He had long since stopped thinking of her as a possession. At times, it seemed as if he belonged to her.

Things went on as before, his life a flow of conflicting feelings, a flow of emotions he could no longer control. It seemed to him, like the stefel dogs that he fed, that he could never really own her. Her alienness was always between them. Her customs were strange, her manner unlike that of his race. And she was guided by this alien quality, this traditional way so unlike his own, to live in a way he could not hope to touch or change. There were certain things between them. She would not eat at the table, eating instead on the floor, after the manner of her people. Then too, like a raccoon on earth, she washed every morsel of food she ate. There was something very animal, very alien about her as she swished a slice of bread in a saucer of water before eating it. He had beaten her for that once, but it made him uncomfortable to see her sitting across the table from him, not eating, staring in the Riyallian way. In a way, it was how she expressed her anger, if indeed she ever experienced it. He sensed her displeasure and once, when he had been particularly cruel, he thought he heard a trilling sound, a throaty vocalization like the death rattle of the stefel dogs. He thought perhaps it was her way of crying. But he could never be sure.

And they had a child, a boy.

Often when the pebble storms of winter kept him inside, he sat before the heating unit watching the boy-child crawling across the floor. She sat motionlessly on the other side of the room like some ill-conceived statue, lost in streams of thought he could never touch, moving with memories he never could share.

He talked her tongue so poorly, he could not make her understand, and she spoke no English, seemingly would not allow herself to learn it. There were times, holding his young son, staring into the child's eyes, blue and single-pupiled like his own, when he wanted to talk to her, to tell her the things and dreams within him. It was never to be.

The days passed silently for them while all around them, like silt deposited by a flooding stream, the immigrants to the planet continued to come. Women, children, entire families moving to Kingane, now safely settled by those who went before them. And as the years rolled by, towns were born, and with them came the civilization that had brought them. Gantry noticed it gradually, the weeks when the trail beyond the end of his land became full of travelers, whereas before he rarely saw more than one or two people a month. One day he stood on the hill behind his cabin and he could see houses going up, maybe two or three miles away, and it was then that he knew a moment of unease, of dread. His own people had caught up with him.

A week later, finding himself dissatisfied, unaccountably restless, he took her into the new town that had sprung up almost overnight just ten miles from his cabin. In a way, his taking her there was a part of the blindness that had grown around him. He'd been with her so long, got so familiar and comfortable around her in their quietly spent years together, it had faded from his mind that she was an alien, that she might not be welcome.

He'd dressed her in a bright dress, purchased from

the harvest buyers who stopped three times a year to buy his harvest of stefel tissue. But he had forgotten her customs, as unchangeable as the blue-green sky above. When they walked across the sidewalks, she followed him, moving behind him at her customary five paces. And in the eyes of those he met, in the eyes of those townspeople, he knew how she would look to them. He felt an anger rising in him. He heard comments from the people on the street, nothing direct, nothing he heard quite clearly, but he knew what they were saying about him, knew what they were thinking about her.

She saw the darkness in his eyes when he turned to look at her, and without a word she turned and walked back to their landcar and got in to wait for him. She took it as she took all things, silently, matter-of-factly. But there was no way she could change who she was. He followed her and got into the landcar, driving away from the town, looking neither to the left nor right but aware that people had moved out of buildings to look at her, to look at them, and it burned into him with a bitterness and a loss that he knew would never stop. And he was never to take her into town again.

He knew then how it would be. When the stefel buyers decided they could no longer afford to visit each stefel rancher individually, when the buyers decided to open up an office in town where the ranchers could bring in their harvest, he knew his life, his aloneness, was lost to him.

At harvest time, when he took his tank, now fitted with wheels, into town to sell his crop of tissue, he could sense the barrier between himself and the others of his kind. As he waited in the outer offices, waiting until his wagon was weighed and unloaded, the others sat apart from him as if he was a man of their race who was somehow not of their race. And the way women of his own kind passed their eyes over him as if he were something unclean filled him with a chill that seized him by the heart.

One day he met Droble at the weighing office, Droble who had two Riyall women. And as Gantry sat there, he listened to the talk around him. The men were talking about the changes around them, about the men who had pioneered this land. The pioneers were sending their Riyall women back into the wild lands from which they had come, sending away their half-breed children, sending them back to their own kind; at least, the ones with any brains were, was what the men said. Droble turned pale as he heard their conversation, the idle chatter of men who had come to this world long after others had made it soft and easy for them. Droble stood up and stalked out of the office with a kind of hurtful violence. Droble still had his two Riyall women. Droble was the kind of man who needed people, a loner who still must be a part of society. Later, as Gantry was picking up his check for his crop, a man ran into the office shouting that Droble had just blown his head off in the middle of the street. The men in the office all dashed out to see it for themselves. Gantry felt all the weight, the hopelessness of his mistakes come crashing down on him. It might have been him out there on the street instead of Droble.

He went home late that morning, very, very drunk. In the morning, the last part of the night, the fatalness of his mistakes was apparent to him. He was no Charlie Droble and he knew that the decision that Droble had made was an easy one compared to the one he knew he would have to make. Couldn't help but make.

But home in his own cabin, watching her and the boy eating, washing their food as was her custom, he found that he did not have the strength to do it. He remembered back to the time before his people had caught up with him. Had she ever really held him tenderly? Was it his imagination that had built her into a person, into a human being? Perhaps she was a fabrication, a cold, emotionless creature he had shaped with his imagination and his great need into more than what she really was. She had never told him that she loved him, for there was no way for her to communicate that, to tell him that. But he had always assumed it, hadn't he? Hadn't the care, the expressionless but gentle caring for the boy convinced him of that?

The winter came, and with it a deep gloom that settled over the little cabin. There was no help for himself, Gantry knew. He was committed to her, to his son, and he could not sever those ties. She in her strange way sensed his great sorrow, and whether comprehending its source or not, seemed to spend more time with the boy, less time with him, a thing that Gantry experienced with a kind of relief. He had found himself very critical of her lately, found himself very quick to notice faults in her, faults that had never seemed obvious to him before.

The meteor shower had lasted two days, longer than any other shower he ever remembered. He sat at the table eating his food, lost in the kind of misery that comes over a child forced to stay inside when it rains and there's nothing to do. He kept running it over and over in his mind, kept staring at them as they ate their meal, washing each bite of food first. The day before, the boy had said his first word. He had sensed it, had sensed that the boy was beginning to take on her personality even though the boy seemed to look a great deal like him. He had understood that first word of his and it was one of her language and not his.

It was funny how that bothered him the most. That the child would speak her words and not his. And it came to him, then, it came to him like a painful tearing sound, and he knew that he could not save himself. He knew he could not save her. There was no hope for her. No hope for him. There was nothing that could be done. Out the window he could see the shells of houses going up at the edge of his land, houses waiting till the summer and the right time to build them. His people had caught up with him.

He got up from the table slowly, his food untouched, and he moved toward them. She knew what was to happen and in that unreadable face, he found the knowledge of what he was about to do. He lifted the boy away from the mat on the floor and cradling him against his chest, turned and walked back to the table. She sat motionlessly in the corner and in that moment he knew, he finally knew she was capable of emotion, that she had feelings of her own.

He pulled a chair up beside his and sat the boy gently down upon the chair. He turned to her, and without a word she knew that the boy's place would hereafter be at the table, she knew it by the sad, unrelenting look on his face.

He took a piece of bread and put it unwashed into the boy's mouth. And then he heard it, and turned to look at her. Her face was turned away, her shoulders motionless.

But he heard it and this time knew what it was. That melodious, birdlike sound, the way the creatures of Kingane cried, the sound the creatures of Kingane made when they were dying.

But he had his back hardened against it and would

not relent, having made the judgment for the boy. But after the way of his own kind, his shoulders shook and he made the harsh, broken rasping sound, the way the creatures of Earth cried, the sound the creatures of Earth made when they were dying.

A Sunday Visit
with Great-grandfather

GREAT-GRANDFATHER stared at his gift with a sharply critical eye. Great-grandmother gnashed her teeth like she always did when great-grandfather was about to make a social error.

"This tobacco stinks!" said great-grandfather. He held the pouch away from his nose. "As usual, my cheap great-grandson has shown his respect by bringing me cheap tobacco."

Great-grandmother kicked great-grandfather in the shin, as she had been doing in such instances as long as she could remember. Not that it did any good. Great-grandfather had grown old and independent and it took something of the magnitude of an earthquake to change his ways.

Great-grandson sighed. He knew that no matter what kind of tobacco he brought or how much it cost, great-grandfather would always say it was cheap.

"You are looking well, great-grandfather," he said.

"A fat lot you know!" said great-grandfather irritably.

"It's the vapors. It gets him in the back," said great-grandmother. "And he hasn't got enough sense to come in when the cold clouds are out. Not him. He stands out in bad vapors and rain looking for a demigod or trying to remember where he's supposed to be, as if one burial rack didn't—"

"Some day your tongue will go crazy and beat you to death!" roared great-grandfather.

Great-grandmother gave her great-grandson a sympathetic look and shrugged.

"How are the white people treating you in away-school?" asked great-grandfather. He shifted his position upon the hard rock so that the sun did not shine directly into his weak, old eyes.

"As badly as usual, revered one. Those white people are crazy."

"And what kind of things are they learning you? Healing arts? Better ways of hunting? Surely these white men are teaching you many things?" said great-grandfather.

"No, great-grandfather," answered great-grandson. "They are not teaching me any of those things. I am learning science. I am learning how lightning is made and what rocks are made of and what stars are and how fast light travels."

"Spells! Most excellent! These white people are smarter than I thought. But what was that you said about light traveling? I have never heard of such a thing! Of what use is it?" great-grandfather asked.

"They are not spells," explained great-grandson patiently. "And the traveling of light is mathematics."

Great-grandfather nodded his head wisely. "Ah, yes! Mathematics." A shadow darkened his face and he scowled.

"What the hell is mathematics?" growled great-grandfather.

"Counting and measuring. Adding and subtracting the number of things one has," said great-grandson.

"Sending you to away-school has turned you into a wise nose! Why didn't you say that the first time! Mathematics! Any fool knows how to count on his fingers! You went to away-school to learn a four-dollar word for counting on your fingers? This is the kind of a thing you are learning?"

"You don't understand. We learn more than just how to count on our fingers. We've learned how to measure great distances. For instance, I know how far away the stars are."

Great-grandfather shook his head. He looked at his wife. They both shrugged. "That is very interesting," said great-grandfather. "And what is that used for?"

"I don't know," admitted great-grandson. "They only told me how far away it is."

"What other kinds of things have they told you?" asked great-grandmother. "These things sound as crazy as eating rocks."

"Well, I have learned that man was once an ape, that the earth flies in the air around the sun and that when people die their bodies rot and their souls go to heaven. Also I learned that—"

Great-grandfather jumped off the rock. "What? What?" he shouted. "What is this craziness! Has my great-grandson fallen upon his head too many times!"

Great-grandmother tried to quiet great-grandfather down but he jumped around like a frightened horse. He paced back and forth, cursing loudly.

"They also told me the Great Spirit is superstition," said great-grandson.

"What is this superstition?" roared great-grandfather. "Is that another of those city funnies you picked up at away-school? If I wasn't so old I'd flatten you with a rock! I never heard such foolishness!"

"But great-grandfather," protested great-grandson, "I am only telling you what they are teaching me at away-school. It isn't my fault that the white people are all crazy. They even told me that it was impossible to talk with people after they are dead."

"They have gone too far!" shrieked great-grandfather. "They have gone too far! There will be no more away-school!"

Great-grandfather beat his scrawny chest with his fists in a defiant gesture which sent him into a fit of coughing.

Great-grandmother patted him on the back as his face swelled up and turned red.

She looked disgusted. "You shouldn't have told him all those terrible things," she said, pounding great-grandfather's back vigorously. "You know this happens every time he gets upset."

Great-grandson looked properly apologetic and helped great-grandmother sit him back on his favorite sitting rock. The coughing fit passed, leaving great-grandfather weak and gasping for breath.

"It's the vapors," said great-grandmother. "If he had enough sense to come in out of the—"

Great-grandfather scowled so ferociously that she stopped speaking. She knew when she was well off.

"No more!" gasped great-grandfather between gasps. "No more away-school!"

"But great-grandfather," the boy protested. "I will be arrested and thrown into the white man's jail if I do not go to away-school."

The old man folded his arms across his chest. He raised his head, tilting it at a defiant angle. He sucked his scrawny stomach in and pushed his thin chest out. It was his warrior's stance, which had once put fear into the hearts of many a comely woman. When great-grandfather did this, it meant that his mind was made up. It meant that there would be no further discussion. It meant that there would be no more away-school. It also meant another coughing spell for great-grandfather, who was always forgetting his condition.

Great-grandmother began whacking him on the back again with the practiced ease of one who has done it many hundreds of times. She sighed. "He never learns."

"Or else he never remembers," suggested great-grandson.

Great-grandmother shook her head wearily. "I think it is a little of both," she said.

The letter from away-school came three weeks later. The boy carried the letter to his great-grandparents. "I told you they were going to throw me into the slammer if I didn't go to away-school," he said after reading them the letter. The letter said they were going to throw him into the slammer.

Great-grandfather started to go into his warrior's stance but the old woman had anticipated that very thing and she whacked him in the back before he could get a decent start at it. He was taken completely by surprise and fell forward off his favorite sitting rock. This saved him from another coughing spell.

"What happens is that they are going to come and get me and throw me in the slammer," said great-grandson, looking unhappy about the whole thing.

"Something will have to be done about this thing," said the old man solemnly from his seat upon the ground.

"I will not take this thing lying down." He got up as if he meant it literally and started to sit back down on his favorite sitting rock. His dim eyes betrayed him and he almost sat down on great-grandmother.

"The rock is two feet to your left," said great-grandmother.

"I knew that all along," said great-grandfather indignantly. "I was only trying to get you to guess my weight."

He moved over to the rock, stared at it carefully, judging its exact location, and sat down. He missed the rock by three inches.

"It is good to sit upon the ground once in a while," reflected the old man as he rubbed his hip. "It gives a man a whole new perspective on things."

Great-grandmother snickered to herself. In an aside to the boy, she said, "Boy! He's in lousy shape, ain't he?"

It was but one day later that great-grandson rushed up to his great-grandparents. "They've come," he cried, gazing over his shoulder fearfully. There was a loud whining noise from the direction from which he had just come. Great-grandfather was asleep in the sun with his mouth open. He jumped awake, thinking he had been shot. He felt all over his chest, not that it would have made any difference in his condition.

"Who? What?" he said.

"The white men have come to throw your one and only great-grandson into the slammer!" shouted great-grandson.

Great-grandfather yawned and closed his eyes again. "That's nice," he said. "I always liked buffalo sou—" He was asleep again.

"Wake up, great-grandfather!" shouted great-grandson.

"Boy, he really is in lousy shape, ain't he?" said great-grandmother.

"Who? What?" said great-grandfather.

"We already covered that already!" groaned great-grandson.

Grudgingly, great-grandfather awoke. He rubbed his eyes. From a distance, there was a strange whooshing noise.

"Who's that whooshing around my place of business!" roared the old man.

"It's the white men come to throw me in the slammer!" yelled great-grandson for the third or fourth time.

"No kidding," said great-grandfather. He didn't seem particularly concerned. "By the way," asked the old man, "what the hell is a slammer?"

"That's a white man's jail," replied the boy.

"Well! Why the hell didn't you say so in the first place! You idiot! I thought a slammer was a—"

Great-grandson was never to know what the old man thought a slammer was because the white men arrived in a strange vehicle without wheels.

"It's the white men come to throw our one and only great-grandson into the slammer," said great-grandmother. But as she said it she had doubts. For one thing, they had tentacles and were blue. She'd seen some ugly white people in her day but none quite as ugly as the two specimens who had just come into view.

Great-grandson threw his hands up in the air, screamed at least once and ran like hell. He disappeared behind an outcropping of rock.

"What's wrong with him?" asked great-grandfather. "Did he sit on a cold worm? Where's he going?"

"It's the white men come to throw our one and only great-grandson into the slammer," repeated great-grandmother, and she motioned at the aliens embarking from the vehicle. He followed her arm with his weak eyes and saw them vaguely.

Great-grandfather snorted. "You think I don't know what they are? I got eyes, you know." He blinked his eyes uncertainly. For some reason, the blurry forms in front of him seemed suspiciously blue. He attributed this to indigestion.

The aliens advanced on the seated couple. The aliens

were six feet tall, covered with blue scaly armor. They had eye bulbs on each side of their faces, thin slit mouths, red eye membranes across red-pupiled eyes. They were clothed in a superior smirk.

"So you think you're going to throw my one and only great-grandson into the slammer, do you?" roared great-grandfather. He immediately went into a coughing fit. Great-grandmother began pumping his back in the usual fashion.

"What's a slammer?" said the first alien. He eyed the old man, who was bent over double, gasping and coughing with his tongue hanging out.

"Boy, he's really in lousy shape, ain't he?" commented the first alien.

"Yeah," said the second alien. "This is going to be easier than making candy out of babies."

The first alien took a hand weapon out of a pouch strapped below his chin. He set the gauge on stun. "This is going to be the easiest one yet. No technology worth shaking a quantum at. No force fields, no personal power packs, no weapons. Clothes made out of animal skins. Primitive." He aimed the weapon at great-grandfather and shot him in the head, laughing to himself all the while.

It had absolutely no effect on the old man. He just kept coughing. The first alien turned and stared at the second alien. "Wow!" he said.

"Yeah," agreed the second alien. A good stun shot

was strong enough to cripple a five-ton herbil.

Great-grandfather coughed, and great-grandmother pounded his back, and great-grandson hid in the rocks, viewing the proceedings with alarm.

"My stunner must be out of whack. Lemme use yours," grunted the first alien.

The second alien handed it over to him. The first alien set it on stun and shot the old man again. Nothing happened. The old man didn't even blink an eye. He was too busy trying to get his breath back.

"Hey!" said the first alien, whipping his tentacles in a confused circle around his shoulders. "Hey!"

The second alien nodded his head. "Yeah."

"Am I gonna get him now!" threatened the first alien, setting his tentacles determinedly around the hand weapon. He set the stunner on full charge, moved the power setting to overload and blasted away at the old man again. The only thing that happened was that the weapon overheated and melted into a shapeless hunk of hot metal. It burned the alien's tentacle. He yelped and threw the useless weapon away. He waved his stinging tentacle in the air. He looked madder than hell. He looked at the second alien, who looked right back at him.

"We didn't get the wrong planet, did we? I mean, I've seen technology and I've seen technology, but this is beyond me. How come he ain't dead, is what I want to know?"

"I can't understand it either," said the second alien. "We flew over the missile base. They had atomic weapons. Real kid stuff. No force fields, no antimatter weapons. Prepubescent technology. So how come this one is so hard to kill?"

"I'll nail him with my molecular disruption gun," said the first alien as he took a small metal tube out of his neck pouch. "He won't know what hit him." He smirked, but his smirk lacked conviction.

Great-grandfather sat weakly on his favorite sitting rock. He'd got his breath back finally. Great-grandmother had her eyes on the ugly white men. She couldn't understand anything they were saying. None of it made any sense. This helped convince her that they were indeed white people.

"Stop burping me!" growled great-grandfather. She stopped whacking his back.

The gun in the alien's tentacles erupted in a silvery-red flash and a brilliant beam of energy passed through great-grandfather and completely destroyed his favorite sitting rock. It disappeared in a shimmering cloud of vaporized molecules. Great-grandfather fell flat on his back. He was so shocked he almost went into another coughing fit.

"Hey!" shouted the first alien, whipping tentacles in all directions, entangling two of them in his confusion. "Hey!"

The second alien was too shocked to even say yeah.

"That does it!" shouted great-grandfather, struggling to get off the ground. "I'm going to teach you crazy white people to mess with me! Throw my one and only great-grandson into the slammer, will you?"

"What's a slammer?" said the first alien. "Are we talking the right language or what?"

"I'm going to hit you with the dreaded curse of Cheroboa! I'll knock your rooty-tooty eyes out!" exclaimed great-grandfather, dangerously close to another coughing fit.

Great-grandmother covered her eyes. "Oh, no! Not that old song and dance again!"

"Maybe they put up that missile base to fool us," suggested the second alien. "Maybe those radio broadcasts we picked up twenty years ago are true? Maybe this guy is Superman?"

"Hoogma nubo toot!" roared great-grandfather, and he made a mystic pass through the air with his hands. He looked around expectantly. Nothing happened.

"Nuts!" he said. "I was sure I had it right."

"Who is kidding whom?" asked the first alien. He eyed the old man critically, studying him first with one eye bulb and then the other.

"Where's his cape? Superman got to have a cape," said the first alien. "How we gonna find out if he's Superman?"

"Hoogma toot nuba." It began raining in downtown

Los Angeles. "Ah, come on now!" complained great-grandfather. "I know I had it right that time!" He stared at the sky expectantly.

The second alien pulled a handful of weapons out of his pouch, rummaging frantically for something at the bottom. He pulled out a hunk of kryptonite and threw it at the old man. They had prepared for everything, even Superman. It passed right through him and fell to the ground.

"He must be the Green Hornet!" said the first alien, all his tentacles agog at the prospect. "Or Captain Marvel! Or all of them!"

"Well, toot hoogma nuba!" roared great-grandfather without much conviction. Suddenly the sky opened up and it began raining frogs.

"Nuts!" said great-grandfather, thoroughly disgusted with the whole business. Frogs pelted off the heads of the aliens. They were too stunned by this sudden turn of events to even duck.

"I give it one more try," said great-grandfather. Great-grandmother, who had been crouching behind her sitting rock, poked her head up from behind the rock and looked rather dubiously at the sky. "He never learns and he never remembers either," she muttered under her breath.

A frog bounced off great-grandfather's head, almost knocking him to the ground.

"And, boy, is he in lousy shape!" she added.

"I heard that," roared great-grandfather, and he went into a violent coughing fit.

The second alien began packing up his weapons meekly. "I think we just better go home and forget about the whole invasion. I think we better leave before he notices we're here and does something to us we'll regret. Did we ever get the wrong planet!"

The first alien was staring at a frog resting on his shoulder. He was scared to death to touch it. He'd heard about warts. The frog returned his stare and then hopped off his shoulder. The alien almost collapsed with relief.

The sky stopped dropping frogs.

"This ain't no technology to be fooling with! Let's get the hell out of here! Man! Am I glad we decided to hit the sticks first!"

"I can't understand it. It should have worked. I can't figure out what went wrong. That curse always worked on chickens," said great-grandfather.

"It could have been worse," said the first alien. "We could have landed in Cleveland."

"Or met the Lone Ranger," added the other alien, a look of pure horror on his face.

The aliens turned in full flight and ran to their vehicle. They jumped in, dropping weapons carelessly in their haste to get away.

"Take a good look," said the first alien as he slammed

the power bar into gear. "Sure doesn't look like a super-technology, does it? I'd swear there wasn't a weapon or self-defense mechanism on any of them. They'll never believe it back home." He stared at great-grandfather with absolute terror. Great-grandfather was looking up into the sky, still expecting the curse of Cheroboa to materialize. "You wouldn't think—" said the first alien, thinking about the energy beams passing through the old man without hurting him at all, thinking about the frogs. "No. No. You wouldn't think—" He paused. "He sure—"

"Is in lousy shape, ain't he?" finished the second alien.

"Yeah," said the first alien. "I should be in such lousy shape!"

They returned to their spaceship and left the Earth as fast as they could travel. They never came back.

"You can come out now!" yelled great-grandmother to great-grandson. "The crazy white men are gone."

"They are?" asked great-grandfather, looking disappointed. "Nuts! Just when I had the curse down pat, too."

Great-grandmother rolled her eyes.

Great-grandson came out from behind a rock. Great-grandfather stared at the rock. "He's putting on weight, ain't he? White man's school has made him fat and weak."

Great-grandmother sighed. It had been a long day.

Every day was a long day that was spent with a rascal like great-grandfather.

"It's time we got some sleep," said great-grandmother.

Great-grandfather yawned.

Great-grandson came up to them and looped an arm in theirs. Lifting them gently to their feet, he walked them across the sacred ground to the burial rack. Tenderly, he helped them climb back onto the burial rack.

"You're a good great-grandson," said great-grandmother. "Will we see you next Sunday?"

"Same time as always," said great-grandson.

"He's such a good great-grandson," said great-grandmother.

"He brings me cheap tobacco," muttered great-grandfather.

Great-grandmother would have kicked him, but he was already snoring.

Mother of Cloth, Heart of Clock

I MEANT to kill him but I had no idea I could do it so completely. I surprised myself. But I guess I lose control sometimes. I go mad, smash things, break out the windows and throw animal droppings at the Sunday crowds. Mad, that's what they think I am. But I don't care what they think, except they're going to kill me. I care about that.

I care about them going to kill me. Wouldn't anyone? Ask anybody else in these cages and they'll all tell you the same thing. Nobody likes to get killed. Except the snakes. Sometimes I wonder if the snakes even know if they're alive or dead. Snakes are an indifferent lot.

Perhaps it's just as well that they kill me. And this time, I hope they do it right. I don't want to go through this again. I'm tired of lying here on this soiled straw matting, at the mercy of my keeper's indigestion. Regular feedings? I should say not. Braddock used to be my keeper; how the crowds loved me then. Fed like clockwork, I was, and sleek and well-petted. The crowds went for me then. I was the fair-haired one then. Yes, sir, no question of it.

But now, since they found Braddock's body partly ingested, the stomach torn out like the sawdust stuffings of a wooden doll, we animals have to take what we can get, which isn't much. Our new keeper, he must be nearly demented, the way he drinks and all, and when his stomach is upset, do we get fed? We do not.

Ever since I killed that man, I guess, things have been bad. I used to be in the same cage with Flippy and Jumpo, but now they've got me penned by myself. Maybe I'm just too old. Getting too old, that's one of the things that is always happening to us. The muscles get stiff and we forget things. One week we can hear the oohs and aahs of the kids watching us and the next, it seems like you can't remember any of the acrobatics and your hair is beginning to fall out. So it goes.

When I was young, I think I was loved. I don't remember my mother, they took her away and gave me this cloth thing with a clock inside. It wasn't the same thing as a mother of course, but it served its purpose. It was better than no mother at all, was the way I looked at it. So soft the cloth was, almost like my mother's fur, and the clock ticking away in as regular a heartbeat as you could like. Of course, every hour the clock gained a minute, which may be the reason why I turned out so wrong. These things happen, you know.

There's still some blood on my straw matting and I really wish someone would come in and change it, but I don't suppose anyone will. Since the murder, no one will come near me except to drop food through the slot in the bars. And not much of that, either. How I miss Braddock. I wish they hadn't found him dead like that. He fed me and fed me well and I'll always remember that about him. He bled terribly when he died. I'll remember that, too. There are so many things to remember.

I miss being petted. Nobody comes to brush me now. I look rather scruffy. Way I look, maybe getting put to death isn't such a bad idea. They don't love me anymore and I don't think they ever will again. Why go on then? What would be the point? I'm too old to do tricks anyway. And I'm so lonely.

I can still see out the high window. I can still climb a little, although what good it does, I don't know. I hear all the people out there laughing and having fun. Living as if nothing had happened, and for them, I guess, nothing has happened. Why did it have to change for me?

Is this what they call growing up? If it is, I don't feel so good and I wish it would go away. Nobody comes to see me. Nothing to look at and nothing to look forward to, one dreary meal a day and not nearly enough to keep me sleek and fit. If they kill me, at least I'll get out of this cage. They'll take me out to bury me. They always bury us in the ground when one of us dies. They have funny ways. I think it is a waste of meat when they bury one of us. Perhaps it does not occur to them that we are edible.

I do not know why they do not eat us when we die. I do not understand them at all. They do so many things that I do not understand. Once they put me in a cage with Nappi. Nappi looked just like me except she seemed to have longer fur and brighter eyes. We used to sleep in the trees, wrapped in each other's arms. We were very happy. But one day they took Nappi to the big white building where they take all the animals that die.

When they brought her back that night, she had funny things made out of glass and metal buried in her head. They had pulled out her hair in two little patches on each side of her head and planted these things in there. I do not know if they thought they would grow there or not. I did not like them. Nappi did not like them either.

Nappi did not like me anymore after that either. She would not climb the tree with me and when I tried to put my arm around her, she sank her sharp white teeth in my arm. I could not go near her without getting bitten. Later they took her away because she tried to bite Braddock when he brought food to us. It was not like Nappi to do that, sweet gentle Nappi, always crowding up to the bars to be first to get petted. She had been one of Braddock's favorites, I know. He always had a good word for her. But she wasn't the same Nappi.

She snarled and raged around the cage. She upset the visitors and so they came and took her one day and I never saw her again. I guess they destroyed her because the things in her head would not grow. I do not understand why they do these things. Nappi was very nice and gentle. She had had a real mother and she seemed so alive.

I sleep a lot because that helps pass the time. I'm really not hungry much anymore and my fur is falling out more and more. I eat when they bring me food but my heart is not in it. I call out to the other animals sometimes at night and they answer, but it does not help very much. I cannot see them and the comfortable sounds they make only make it seem worse.

I did not mean to kill that man. I did not know who he was. He shouldn't have been here. Perhaps I did mean to kill him. He frightened me. Yes, he did, and I guess that is why I killed him. There was something not right that night when he came to my cage. All the other animals sensed it, too. They were pacing restlessly in their cages, moaning and growling. Some of the big cats threw themselves against the bars, roaring.

The man smelled strange. He smelled like the animals that get sick and are taken away to the white building after they stop moving. Sometimes the animals would lay there all night sick like that and not moving before the attendants found them. The smell would get very strong then. That was the kind of smell the man had.

It was dark, I was awake in my tree, huddled against the trunk, missing the comforting warmth of Nappi, when he came over the wall. He fell to this side of the wall. He was very clumsy. It was frightening the way he fell. Like he did not have any bones. He just collapsed like jelly, rolled and then slowly got to his feet. He frightened me.

I hid in the tree. I did not want him to see me. He walked very stiffly. Every step he took, it seemed like he was going to fall over. His eyes were closed, I could see that in the full light of the moon, and he reminded me of some of the animals who move their legs and make noises in their sleep.

I hid behind my tree trunk and I thought he would not find me. But I was wrong. He was coming for me. He came to the door of my cage and his hands brushed over the locks. The animals in the cages next to mine were in a rage. Their screams and catcalls filled the air. The man did not seem disturbed.

I was getting frightened. I get angry when I get frightened, and I do things. I do not like to do things, but when I am frightened I lose control. The man was tearing at the hinges of the door to my cage. I did not want him to come in. His smell frightened me.

He forced the door open. I bared my teeth and growled. I didn't want him in my cage. I don't like it when people come into my cage. His eyes opened, but his eyes were glassy. I do not think he could see me. I growled.

His mouth twitched and his lips moved. He reached up through the branches and his hand touched my leg. His hand was cold and damp and I couldn't stand the smell. I jumped down at him. I bit his face and tore at his eyes and jumped up and down on his chest when he fell over. He fell over very easily and he did not make a sound or fight back. That made me even madder and I tore away at him with my sharp white teeth.

He came apart. The other animals in the cages next to mine were roaring and throwing themselves against the bars of their cages in frenzy. I went wild, too. I was frightened and I lost control. I bit the bad-smelling thing's head off. I sank my teeth again and again into its soft white neck and it fell off and I worried the bloody thing across the floor. I clawed its foul-smelling clothes off, ripping it into shreds, and stamped furiously on the soft white body. I was frightened and angry.

Then I ran up the tree and hugged the branches until

my arms hurt, and then I rested and calmed down. I was tired and frightened and I wanted to go away from there and not see that man anymore. I looked down and the man had not gone away so I stayed up there in the tree and hugged the branches.

All the man's arms and legs had come off and I had got blood on my straw and I did not like it. I don't like blood. It makes my head hurt and I get angry and frightened. I stayed up in the tree all night.

When the new keeper, the mean one who drank, came in the morning to change my straw he found the dead man. I thought he was going to hit me with a stick. But he didn't hit me. He ran away and they came with a net and dragged me out of the tree and wrapped me up in the net and no matter how much I screamed, they wouldn't listen. I wanted to be free and they wouldn't listen.

That's why they put me in this cage in the big white building and why the men in the white coats are going to kill me. They keep telling me they are going to kill me but I don't care. My fur is falling out and they don't feed me enough and nobody pets me anymore. I don't care. I'll sleep a lot and that will help pass the time. They don't love me anymore. I don't care. I'll sleep a lot and have good dreams and I will be very angry when they wake me up because my dreams will be very pleasant and I will not want to leave them.

I will dream that I am dead.

The Bleeding Man

THE MEDICINE shaker, the bone breaker. I have seen and been all these. It is nothing but trouble.

I have sat on the good side of the fire. I have cried over young women. It is nothing but trouble.

Miss Dow leaned against the observation window. Her stomach revolted and she backed away. Unable to quell the nausea rising within her, she clamped a hand to her mouth.

Dr. Santell gently took her arm, led her away from the window and helped her to a couch facing away from the observation window.

Nausea passed; Miss Dow smiled weakly. "You did warn me," she said.

Dr. Santell did not return the smile. "It takes getting used to. I'm a doctor, and immune to gore, but still I find it unsettling. He's a biological impossibility."

"Not even human," Miss Dow suggested.

"That's what the government sent you here to decide," said Dr. Santell. "Frankly, I'm glad he's no longer my responsibility."

"I want to look at him again."

Santell shrugged, lit a syntho. Together they walked back to the observation window. He seemed amused at her discomfort.

Again, Miss Dow peered through the window. This time it was easier.

A young man, tall and well-muscled, stood in the middle of the room. He was naked. His uncut black hair fell to the small of his back.

His chest was slit with a gaping wound that bled profusely; his legs and stomach were soaked with blood.

"Why is he smiling? What is he staring at?" she asked, unable to take her eyes off the figure before her.

"I don't know," said Dr. Santell. "Why don't you ask him?"

"Your sense of humor escapes me," said Miss Dow through tightly closed lips.

Dr. Santell grinned and shrugged. His synthetic cigarette reached the cut-off mark and winked out. The butt flashed briefly as he tossed it into the wall disposal.

"Doesn't everything?" suggested Dr. Santell, trying not to laugh at his little joke.

Miss Dow turned away from the window. Her look was sharp, withering. "Tell me about him," she snapped, each word like ice. "How did he get—that way?"

His amusement faded. He licked his lips nervously, nodded. "He has no name, at least no official name. We call him Joe. Sort of a nickname. We gave him that name about—"

"Fascinating," interrupted Miss Dow, "but I didn't come here to be entertained by some droll little tale about his nickname."

"Friendly, aren't you?" asked Santell dryly. A pity, he thought. If she knew how to smile she might have seemed attractive.

"The government doesn't pay me to be friendly. It pays me to do a job." Her voice was cold, dispassionate. But she turned to face Dr. Santell in such a way that she would not see the bleeding man. "How long has he been like this?"

"It's all in my report. If you'd like to read it I could—"

"I'd prefer a verbal outline first. I'll read your report later; I trust that it is a thorough one." She eyed him sharply.

"Yes, quite thorough," Dr. Santell replied, the polite edge in his voice wearing thin.

He turned away from Miss Dow, gazed in at the bleeding man. His words were clipped, impartial. "He is approximately twenty-three years old and has been as he is now since birth."

"Incredible!" said Miss Dow, fascinated in spite of herself. "All this is documented?"

"Completely. There is no possibility of fakery. Nor point either, for that matter."

"Just as you say," echoed Miss Dow. "What have you done to try to cure it? Is it some form of stigmata?"

Dr. Santell shook his head. "If this is stigmata, it is the most extreme case this world will ever see. Besides, it is inconceivable that a psychosomatic illness could cause such a drastic biological malfunction."

"But surely some sort of surgery—?" began Miss Dow. "Some sort of chemical therapy would—"

Dr. Santell shook his head emphatically. "We've tried them all in the seven years he's been here. Psycho-chemistry, primal reconditioning, biofeedback—tried singly and together; none have had any effect. He's a biological impossibility."

"What is his rate of bleeding?" she asked.

"It varies," said Dr. Santell. "Somewhere between two and three pints an hour."

"But it's not possible!" exclaimed Miss Dow. "No one can—"

"He can and does," interrupted Dr. Santell. "He doesn't do anything normally. I can give you ten reasons why he should be dead. Don't ask me why he isn't."

Miss Dow turned her head around and stared at the silent figure standing in the center of the room. The bleeding man had not moved. The blood flowed evenly from the chest wound, gathering in a coagulating pool at his feet.

"I've had enough." She turned away from the window. "Show me to my office. I'm ready to read that report now."

Two hours later, the last page of Dr. Santell's report slipped from nerveless fingers. The bleeding man lay outside the parameters of human biology. By all rights he should have been dead; indeed, could never have lived. Her hands were a little unsteady as she punched in Dr. Santell's office on the videophone. His face appeared on the screen—and it was flushed.

"Report to me immediately," Miss Dow snapped.

"I doubt it, sweetheart," said Dr. Santell, grinning. "I'm off the case, remember?" He drank something out of a dark tumbler.

"You're drinking!" snapped Miss Dow.

"Now that you mention it," admitted Dr. Santell agreeably. He gave her a lopsided grin. "Perhaps you would care to join me?"

"You are a disgusting, undisciplined lout. And I should like to remind you that you are still responsible to me. You may be discharged from this case in your professional capacity, but your standing orders are to cooperate with me in any way possible."

"So I'm cooperating," muttered Dr. Santell. "I'll stay out of your way, you stay out of mine."

"I won't tolerate this!" she raged. "Do you realize to whom you are talking?"

Dr. Santell thought that over slowly. His face tightened. He did realize who she was. It sobered him a little. He took another drink from the tumbler to compensate.

"Are you sober enough to answer a few questions?"

He thought that over for a while too. "I'm drunk enough to answer any questions you have. I don't think I could answer them sober," he said.

"I am trying to be understanding," said Miss Dow, a note of conciliation in her voice. "I realize it is quite natural for you to resent me. After all, I am responsible for your termination at this installation."

Dr. Santell shrugged it off. He took another drink from the tumbler.

"We're both professionals, Dr. Santell," reasoned Miss Dow. "We can't let emotional considerations enter into this. There is no place for emotion here. Our goals must be—"

"Hell! That's easy for you to say!" growled Dr. Santell. "You don't have any!"

"That's quite enough, thank you," said Miss Dow, pressing her lips together in a tight, angry line.

"No, it's not enough—" started Dr. Santell. "You can't—"

"The subject is closed!" she shouted.

There was an uneasy silence.

Miss Dow broke it by changing the subject. "What about his parents?" she asked.

"Didn't you read my report?"

"It said they committed suicide. It did not specify or go into any details. I have to know more than that. Your report was supposed to be thorough. You didn't list your sources of information on his early life, for one thing. I need to know—"

"Ask Nahtari. He can tell you everything," he said. He shrugged as if to say it was out of his hands.

"Who?"

"Nahtari. His uncle. He comes every week to visit his nephew. Nahtari used to exhibit him at the carnival until we discovered him and brought him here. If you'll turn to the financial report near the back, you will see that we pay him a small gratuity for the privilege of studying his nephew. We pay him by the week and he stops in to pick up his check and talk to his relative."

"Did you say he talks to his relative?"

"Yeah. It's pretty strange. Nahtari talks to Joe every

week for an hour. I don't know if Joe understands any-thing that is said to him or even if Nahtari cares if he understands. I've never heard Joe respond in any way, not in the seven years I've been here."

"When does this Nahtari make his weekly visit?"

"He's here now in my office. He brings me a pint of whiskey every week. Makes it himself. You'd never be-lieve how good—"

Miss Dow hit the dial-out button viciously, cutting him off in mid-sentence.

She pushed open the door to Dr. Santell's office. She hadn't bothered to knock. Dr. Santell had his feet propped up on the edge of his desk. He held a drink in one hand and a deck of cards in the other. Across the desk from him sat a gray-headed Indian dressed in faded blue jeans, cracked leather boots and a tattered flannel shirt.

"I'll see your dime and raise you a dime," said Dr. Santell, slamming a dime onto the pile of change on the desk between them.

"Are you Nahtari?" demanded Miss Dow, coming into the room. The two studiously ignored her.

"It depends," said the old Indian, not looking up from his cards. "I'll meet your dime and raise you a quarter."

Dr. Santell bit his lip. "You're bluffing! I know you don't have that other ace!"

Miss Dow marched up to the desk, snatched the cards out of Dr. Santell's hands.

Dr. Santell pounded his desk in anger. "Stupid bitch! I had him beat!" He tried to collect the torn cards in his lap.

"Is she some kind of nut?" asked Nahtari, holding his cards out of harm's way.

Dr. Santell dumped the torn pieces of cards on the top of the desk and sighed. "Yeah. A government nut. She's in charge of Joe now."

Nahtari scowled and laid his cards face up on the desk. "And that means she wants to ask me about my relative."

"It certainly does," said Miss Dow. "Would you like to come to my office?"

Nahtari shrugged. There seemed to be no way to avoid it.

"You are owing me twelve dollars," he said to Dr. Santell as he rose to leave the room.

"Don't I always," growled Dr. Santell, staring at the ace that Nahtari had had after all.

"Sit down, Nahtari. This may take a while. I have a great many questions I want to ask you." She put a new cartridge in her tape machine and turned it on.

"If Dr. Santell had taken down all facts from before when I tell him I would not having to be saying again," said Nahtari. "I get tired of telling the story and having no one taking down so I don't have to do all over again."

Miss Dow patted the tape machine. "Don't worry about it," she assured him. "This recorder will make a permanent record of everything you say. I guarantee you won't have to tell it again."

"You going to listen and take down no matter what?"

"Every word," she replied.

She started to ask a question but Nahtari held up his hand. "Let me tell whole story," said Nahtari. "It will be a saving of time and you can ask questions after if you have any. I want to get this over before too long. Got to catch Dr. Santell before he leave with my twelve dollars."

Nahtari scratched his chest over his right shirt pocket.

"That sounds all right to me," agreed Miss Dow. "Could you start with his parents? I'd like to know—"

"He killed them."

"What?" Miss Dow was stunned.

"He killed them," repeated Nahtari matter-of-factly. "I was there the day he was born. His father and mother died within an hour of his birthing. He killed them."

Miss Dow was confused. "But how did it happen? How could—"

"You was not going to ask questions until I finished," accused Nahtari, dragging the back of his hand insolently across his nose.

Miss Dow settled back into her seat with a tight-lipped smile. She motioned for him to continue.

"His parents were medicine people. They were people of great power. My brother was one of the strong ones. They had this child stronger than them."

Miss Dow made a face. "You don't expect me to believe in primitive super—"

"I am expecting of you to keep your stupid mouth shut so this telling can be done and over with. I want to tell this so you will no longer pester me when I come to see my relative. I know all of your kind of government people. You harass a person—"

"Tell the story!" rasped Miss Dow. "For Christ sakes, just tell the story!" She drummed her fingers impatiently on the desk.

"My brother and his woman were filled with the sickness of the world. I knew that my brother did not want to live. His wife knew this and was content to go with him. Then when they had decided the road, she became heavy with child. They had no expecting of this. They became uncertain and did not know the way. But they could not change their decision for the living of the child. They went into the mountains, looking for their road. It was in the fifth month of the child in her belly."

Miss Dow sighed impatiently and settled back in her chair. It looked to be a long story, unrestricted by the inclusion of anything factual. Already she regretted asking him for information.

"They were high in the mountains. They laid down for dying but something strange happened. The child began speaking to them. The child was angry. They ran to the high places, to throw themselves off before the power of the child got too strong for them. But the child stopped them at the edge of the cliff and turned them around. The child forced them back down the mountain. And for four months, they were prisoners of the child."

"Are you seriously telling me that—" began Miss Dow with disgust.

Nahtari snorted contemptuously and passed his hands in front of his eyes. His eyes seemed to be focused on some far horizon. His voice mocked hers. "I just had a vision. I saw you and Dr. Santell embraced upon the ground and then suddenly crushed by a falling outhouse."

"I'm not laughing," said Miss Dow. She wasn't laughing.

"Somebody is," said Nahtari with a straight face. "I knew you was going to not let me finish the story and take it all down so I don't have to tell it again. Nobody ever lets me finish my story," complained Nahtari.

"Christ! I don't blame them!" said Miss Dow. "I've

never heard such an outrageous piece of trash." She turned the tape machine off. "You may have all the time in the world, but I haven't got time to listen to this idiocy!" She stood up and marched around the desk. "When you leave, shut the door."

Nahtari came around the desk and sat down in her chair. He tilted the chair back and rested his bootheels on the desk. He turned the tape-recorder microphone around so that it pointed at him. He pushed the recording button and began talking into the machine.

"You bet this time, record is made of all the facts," he said, and went on with the story. "For four months, they were prisoners of the child. Five days before he was born, the child began to fear leaving the belly. The fear did not last long, but it lasted long enough for his father to put poison in their food without the child's knowing. They ate this poison, the mother, the father and the child.

"The child felt the poison and changed it into water in his belly. He felt great sadness in his heart and an anger because they did not want him to live. They did not want him born into a world they had grown sick of. It was not their right to choose for him because his power was greater than theirs. He did not change the poison flowing through them to water. His hatred was at them for they had let the world beat them. They began the agony of poison dying, but they could not die.

"I sat with them through this time. I sat with my brother and my sister by law and they told me these things through their agony. They screamed to die but the child was punishing them for letting the world beat them. I, Nahtari, did not want to see the child born into this world. I feared his coming. There was nothing I could do. He came to birth.

"It was not a child like expected. He bled. His chest was bleeding. I had expected hot roaring fires. I had expected a child of frightful appearance. It was but a small baby that bled and could not talk.

"The father pulled the baby up and beat him into breathing. He laid the baby on the bed and went outside the house. After a little while, my sister by law got to her feet, swaying on dizzy legs, and she staggered out after him. I tried to stop the bleeding of the baby chest but I was too scared about my brother and sister by law. I ran outside. They laid side by side in the black dirt of the garden. They were dead and five days decayed.

"I took the little one into my home, but the bleeding sickened my old woman and she died. So I took the bleeding one to the traveling show. The white people there did not sicken and die at the sight of his bleeding.

"In lines all around the tent they would stand to pay good money to see the bleeding one. They all wanted to see him bleeding and they were not sickened by it and they did not die. But the government people came and took the bleeding man from me and made me sign little pieces of paper and gave me money so they could do what they do. I turned him over to the government ones and that is all there is to the story and it is the truth.

"Now I come every week to talk to him. I know he is too powerful to have a name. I am waiting for him. I am telling so I will not have to tell it again and so that this warning is given to all who would have dealings with him. He is not ready to do what he will one day do. Do not walk in his shadow. Leave him alone, for he is not you. For twenty-three years he has been gathering power. That is all I have to say."

He switched off the tape machine, smiling to himself because there was no one to hear it. He closed the door carefully behind him and went looking for Dr. Santell and his twelve dollars.

Miss Dow pushed open the door cautiously. She was not sure if she had the stomach for what she was doing. But making up her mind, she stepped into the room. She kept telling herself that he was perfectly harmless.

The drain in the center of the floor was stopped up with clotted blood. He stood in a shallow pool of his own blood. His body was motionless, his breathing just barely perceptible by a slight rising and falling of his chest. The blood flowed steadily to the floor.

"Can you hear me?" she asked nervously. She shut the door behind her. She kept her eyes on his face. He stared at her but gave no sign that he had heard her. He seemed to be in no pain, despite the stream of blood flowing down his chest.

"I'm not going to hurt you." She approached him slowly with a small glass lab beaker. Averting her eyes slightly, she placed the glass container below the wound. She felt a little foolish for having spoken to him. It was obvious to her now that he was little better than a cretin and that he could not understand a word she said.

She stood there awkwardly, the glass beaker filling with his blood. The naked man seemed unaware of her presence, yet still she felt an unreasonable fear. There was something frightening about the still figure. Something threatening, otherworldly in the steady flow of blood down his chest. He did not seem vulnerable. Rather it was as if the world were too insignificant for him to notice it.

She backed away with a full glass of his blood. She felt better with each step she took. He stared at her, no expression on his face, his eyes unusually bright. She had felt very uncomfortable under his stare.

Miss Dow had turned and started out the door, watching him all the while. Suddenly he moved. She turned quickly. Fear rose in her like a tide. The bleeding man cupped a hand beneath the wound in his chest.

Slowly, he brought his hands to his lips and drank. Miss Dow fainted.

Dr. Santell found her in the doorway. A tiny red pool of fresh blood was beginning to blacken on the floor beside her head. The glass beaker she had brought into the room was gone. "What happened?" asked Dr. Santell, bending over the couch, his voice oddly gentle despite its gruffness. "Here—take a sip of this," he said, offering her a small glass of whiskey. "It'll steady your nerves."

She was too weak to refuse. The whiskey burned her throat and made her cough. He made her take another sip. It almost made her gag, but seemed to help. A touch of color reappeared in her face.

"He—he—he drank his own blood!" she whispered, tottering on the edge of hysteria.

Dr. Santell leaned forward eagerly. His features sharpened, his manner became intent and forceful. "Are you sure?" he demanded.

"Yes, I'm sure," she said with a trace of her normal sharpness.

"Are you sure—absolutely sure—he drank his own blood?" he asked again, impatiently. The answer seemed unusually important to him.

"Of course, I'm sure, damn it! It was absolutely disgusting!" She wrinkled up her nose. "That revolting animal did it on purpose! Just because I collected a beaker of—"

Dr. Santell suddenly became greatly agitated. "You collected a glass of blood?" he asked.

She nodded, bewildered by his strange behavior.

"God! It's happened again," he muttered. "It's happened again!" A look of dread passed over his face.

"What the devil are you talking about?" demanded Miss Dow.

"When I heard you scream, I started running. I was the first one to reach you. You were sprawled in the doorway. There was a big bloodstain beside your head on the floor. There was no glass on the floor of the room and it wasn't in the hallway."

"Don't be ridiculous! I had it with me. Isn't this an awfully big fuss to be making over a—"

Dr. Santell turned his back on her and dialed security.

"Hobeman? This is Santell. Have room 473 searched for a glass beaker. Delay his feeding time if you have to, but find that beaker!" He shut off the view screen.

He looked at Miss Dow. Her face was blank with bewilderment. Before she could ask a question he began. "Something strange has developed in the last few weeks. Our monitors have been picking up unusual activity levels. They aren't sophisticated enough to tell us exactly what's happening but his heartbeat and galvanic skin responses have been fluctuating wildly."

"But what does that have to do with the glass?" asked Miss Dow.

"I'm coming to that. A week ago, during one of his strange activity levels, the observation port on the wall of his room disappeared."

Miss Dow's face registered shock. "Disappeared? How is that possible?"

Dr. Santell was grim. "I have no idea. We found traces of melted glass on the floor of the room. But what disturbs me the most is that we could detect no coronary activity. For two hours his blood was circulating, but his heart wasn't functioning."

"He's not human, is he?" said Miss Dow.

"I don't know," said Dr. Santell, staring off into space. "I just don't know."

He pushed the carts through the door. The bleeding man stared at him as he had stared for the seven years he had been there.

"Soup's on, Joe," said the man with the feeding carts.

Two men hidden from view by the door were examining two streaks of melted glass on the floor.

"Hey, hold up there," said one of the men. "He's not to be fed until we've finished our search."

"I won't get in the way. What's disappeared this time?"

"Nothing important," grumbled one of the men. "Just a glass jar from the lab."

"Shame on you, Joe," said the cartman, waving a finger at the motionless figure in the center of the room. "You oughtn't to be stealing stuff like that." He opened the top of his cart and took out a pair of gloves.

"It won't hurt if I feed him, will it? I don't have to hose him down until you guys have finished," he said, pulling the gloves over his hands.

"Go ahead. We aren't going to find anything anyway."

The cartman opened a panel on the side of the cart and brought out a bowl of raw meat. He sat it on the floor in front of the bleeding man. From the other cart he got a large bowl of uncooked vegetables and a large wooden ladle.

He detached a water hose from the wall and started backing toward the bleeding man, uncoiling the hose as he walked. When he got to the end of the hose, he turned around.

The bleeding man had overturned the feeding bowls with his feet. He was drinking his own blood from cupped hands.

"This is what you are looking for," said Dr. Santell, handing Miss Dow a clipboard. "His blood type is O lateral. We've run hundreds of tests on it and it seems to be perfectly normal blood, a little more resistant to some diseases than ordinary blood but otherwise normal. It's too bad the government won't let us use his blood. He's a universal donor and at the rate he produces blood, I'll bet he could supply Intercity all by himself."

"But that's just the point. We *are* going to use his blood," said Miss Dow. "We are going to use a lot more besides. That's why I was sent here."

"The government's changed its policy then?" asked Dr. Santell. "Why?"

"We've given transfusions of his blood to prisoners and it seems to have no bad effects. Tell me, you've studied him for seven years. Do you have any idea how something like him is possible?"

Dr. Santell lit a synthetic cigarette slowly. He gave her a curious look.

"Did you listen to Nahtari's explanation?"

"That lunacy," sniffed Miss Dow. "I think we should pay a little more attention to a chromosomal mutation theory than some wild story from some primitive like Nahtari."

Dr. Santell shrugged. "It doesn't really matter what caused it. I couldn't even make an educated guess. His version is the only evidence we have."

"Confine yourself to specifics, please," said Miss Dow. "What biological evidence do we have?"

"There is biological evidence pointing to chromosomal differentiation. He has sixty-four paired chromosomes. I have been unable so far to determine their exact structure. He seems to have all the normal ones. Technically, that makes him a member of our species, I suppose. But it's those extra chromosomes that are so unusual. They seem to be entirely new structures, unlike anything we are familiar with. It must be something outside our experience. I think I pointed this out in more detail in my report."

"But technically, he is human?" asked Miss Dow.

"I would say he is," said Dr. Santell.

"Very well. Then I am going to give the final go-ahead on this project," said Miss Dow.

"And what project is that?"

"We're going to transfer him to the military dome at Intercity where he will be dissected for tissue regeneration. Hopefully, his cellular matrix will produce like functioning biological constructs."

"What!" Dr. Santell jumped to his feet. "You're not serious! That would be murder! Matrix reconstruction from tissue cultures has never advanced beyond the experimental stage! We don't have the technology to stimulate the reproduction of brain and nerve tissue! Good lord, woman, you can't seriously—"

"I am quite aware of our shortcomings in the field of tissue regeneration," said Miss Dow coldly. "For years, our work in this area has been little better than a waste of time and materials. We have yet to produce a successful unit with a well-developed nervous system. Nor have we been able to successfully clone an individual. These matters, however, are not relevant to this case."

"Not relevant! You'll kill him! And to what purpose? A line of research that you yourself admitted has been a waste of time!" stormed Dr. Santell, his face flushed with anger.

"Be careful, Dr. Santell," she cautioned him. "I don't think I am happy with your choice of words. We are not going to kill him. Many of our first tissue-regeneration experiments are still alive—alive after a fashion, that is. Their bodies still function, their cells still grow, it is only their minds that are dead." She smiled.

"It's still murder! You have no right!" Dr. Santell looked away from Miss Dow. He had suddenly realized that the things he was saying could be considered treason.

"When's the last time you had an attitude check, Dr. Santell?" asked Miss Dow. "I almost thought I heard you say something that was opposed to the wishes of our government. You did agree that my patient can be made ready for transport tomorrow morning, didn't you?"

"Of course," said Dr. Santell. "He will be ready."

"And did I hear you use the word *murder*, Dr. Santell? I *did* hear you use the word! I'm sure General

Talbot will be most interested in your attitude."

Dr. Santell turned and began walking out of the room. He knew that he was in trouble and nothing he could say would make it any better.

"Dr. Santell!"

He turned to look at her.

"I'm really not hard to get along with," said Miss Dow. "You have the reputation of being a brilliant scientist. I've handled your type before. I am willing to overlook a small measure of eccentricity. But I draw the line at treason."

His expression remained blank.

"It's only natural that you're defensive about your patient after seven years," she soothed. "You have personalized him, lost your objectivity. But you must know as well as I do that the bleeding man is a brainless vegetable, hopelessly retarded since birth. You can see that, surely?"

Dr. Santell stared wordlessly.

"It would be a lot easier for me," she continued, "if I had your cooperation on this thing. You've had seven years' experience on this project and you could help us smooth over any rough spots we might encounter. This isn't exactly a normal case. It will require special procedures. Procedures that your cooperation will make possible." She smiled at him. "My report could be a very positive one. It depends on you."

Dr. Santell forced himself to smile. "Believe me," he said, "I shall cooperate in any way I can. I apologize for my behavior."

Miss Dow nodded. "Good. Now, how much blood could, let's say, ten of his regenerations produce in a forty-eight-hour period?"

Dr. Santell began punching up figures on his desk calculator.

The bleeding man continued to drink. The men studying the glass streaks on the floor had fled.

A security guard unlocked the door and looked into the room. The bleeding man did not seem aware of the other's presence. A call went out for Dr. Santell.

Dr. Santell, followed by Miss Dow, arrived just in time to see the heavy door buckling outward.

"He's gone berserk!" screamed Miss Dow as the door was battered off its hinges. The bleeding man walked through the wreckage of the door. He advanced upon them, a crimson trail of blood behind him on the floor. Miss Dow fled, screaming. Dr. Santell stood his ground. The bleeding man brushed him lightly as he walked past. He looked neither to left nor right. He strode down the corridor, moving quickly, relentlessly.

Dr. Santell ran in front of him and tried to push him to a halt. His hands slipped, coming away blood-soaked. His efforts to stop him were futile. Through the plasti-glass corridor walls he could see the security guards gathering around Miss Dow at the corridor exit. Dr. Santell took hold of the bleeding man's arm and tried to drag him to a stop, but found himself being dragged instead. The bleeding man did not even break stride.

Miss Dow stood within a cordon of security men. Dr. Santell knew what she would order them to do even before the bleeding man smashed through the exit door.

"Aim for his head!" she shouted.

A burst of stunner fire took the bleeding man full in the face. He walked several steps, then toppled.

Dr. Santell rushed to his side and put a hand on his chest. "He's still alive," he muttered to himself.

"Good shooting, men," congratulated Miss Dow. "A couple of you carry the body down to the lab."

"Is there very much damage to his head?" she asked. "Is he still alive? Not that it matters. We can't risk another episode like this. We might as well do the dissection here. It'll make him easier to handle. We'd have to ship him frozen anyway, now that we know more about his capabilities."

The security men carried the body away.

"He's still alive," Dr. Santell said, pronouncing each word slowly and distinctly. "He's very much alive."

Miss Dow had a surgical gown on and a mask. "Are you sure you can handle the dissection all by yourself,

Dr. Santell? I could fly someone in to assist."

"Quite sure," said Dr. Santell, bending over the still form on the surgery table. "I'll begin soon. You'd better leave now."

"I'll be waiting at the military base in Intercity for the body," said Miss Dow. She came over to the table and stood beside him. Her voice was cold and emotionless, as usual. "You realize I still must report your treasonable remarks to General Talbot."

Dr. Santell nodded, not looking in her direction.

"However, your behavior has shown marked improvement. That too will be noted in my report. Trying to stop this creature single-handedly in the corridor like you did was a very brave if somewhat foolish thing to do. You realize, of course, that the matter is out of my hands. General Talbot will be the one deciding, not I. Perhaps, after a short period of retraining, you may even be reassigned. A man of your reputation, I'm sure, will find it very easy to rejoin the fold. Only a fool—or a traitor—bucks the system."

Dr. Santell seemed not to be listening. He stuck a needle into the arm of the body on the dissection table.

"What a shame a body like that should have no mind," mused Miss Dow. "Just think of the power he must have in order to smash through those doors like he did."

"Yes," Dr. Santell replied tonelessly.

Miss Dow pulled her mask off and turned to leave.

"Wait," said Dr. Santell. "Before you go, could you hand me that box of clamps under the table here?"

She bent over and looked under the table. "I don't see any—"

His scalpel sliced through her right carotid artery. Her body jerked convulsively and she crashed heavily to the floor.

"Yes," said Dr. Santell with a strange look on his face. "It is always a shame to find a good body with a defective mind."

It took him a little over two hours to dissect her. By the time he finished, the stimulant he had injected into him had brought the bleeding man back to consciousness.

As he was putting her dismembered body into the liquid nitrogen packs for shipping, he kept his eyes on the body of the bleeding man. The body sat up slowly and opened its eyes. The head swiveled and the eyes regarded him. The eyes were alive with raw intelligence. The body slid off the table gracefully and stood up, the wound on his chest completely healed.

"I knew," said Dr. Santell. "I knew."

The medicine shaker, the bone breaker. I have seen and been all these. It is nothing but trouble.

I have sat on the good side of the fire. I have cried over young women. It is nothing but trouble.

These are the words I heard written in his skin. He made me kill her. I had to do it. I am not sorry. I knew. That is enough, knowing.   —Paul Santell

(*This suicide note was found near the charred body of Dr. Santell, who, Intercity Police say, apparently soaked himself with an inflammable liquid and then set himself afire. Dr. Paul Santell, twice recipient of the Nobel Prize in psycho-chemistry, had been experiencing . . . . —excerpt from* Intercity Demographic Area Telepaper.)

The bleeding man, cured of bleeding, walked without haste toward the door leading outside. He remembered the taste of blood, he who no longer had need of it. He pushed the door open and stepped outside. The sky pulled at him, but he resisted for that last little moment. His feet touched the ground. His lungs filled with air. His eyes danced on the horizons of the world. Raising his hands into the air, he let the sky pull him away from the earth. He took the air in his lungs and thrust it out with a shout. Silently his lips formed words.

And then he had no more need of air and words. His fingers curled into the hands of the sky. He disappeared in a cloud.

He Who No Longer Bleeds is gone. He will return. To bleed again.